MY SOUL TO REAP

RENEE JOINER

OSHUN
Publications

My Soul to Reap © Copyright 2020 by Renee Joiner

ISBN: 978-1-950378-45-6

Book Design by Saruuh Kelsey

www.lskcoverdesign.com

Published by Oshun Publications

www.oshunpublications.com

Contents

Did you know you can take every story with you?

I know it's tough these days to simply find the time to relax and curl up with a good book. This is why I'm delighted to share that I have books available in audio book format.

Best of all, you can get the audio book version of any book by me for free as part of a 30-day Audible trial.

Members get free audio books every month and exclusive discounts. It's an excellent way to explore and determine if audio book learning works for you.

If you're not satisfied, you can cancel anytime within the trial period. You won't be charged, and you can even keep your audio book.

To choose a free audio book, click on your favorite title's cover to be taken to Audible's website for details.

Remember, there's no obligation to buy.

reneejoinerauthor.com/audiobooks

JOIN MY NEWSLETTER

GET UPDATES, FREEBIES & GIVEAWAYS

RENEEJOINERAUTHOR.COM/NEWSLETTER

More Books by Renee

Singles
Half Demon
Wanted Undead or Alive

ONE

The Soul That Would Not Leave

SABINE DUBOIS COULD REMEMBER TAKING A DEEP BREATH, filling herself with resolve. That was to be the day, and she had decided there was no going back. Besides, Sabine had already promised her aunt that she would finally join the family business on a full-time basis. So, she had marched into her old boss's office and quit, explaining how she needed to join the family business as her aunt needed her.

She had felt so excited on her last day of working at her old job as she packed up. She had felt so sure that would be the last day of high stress, too much coffee, and chewed-off nails. That it would be the last day of getting stuck in peak hour traffic for hours on end. Sitting trapped in her car, tucked between all that frustration and blaring horns as each car moved by at a snail's pace.

Moving into the family business was supposed to be a lot less stressful. Yet, here she was with chewed-off nails, heading into the dark hills as the clock raced towards midnight. She had traded peak hour traffic for midnight runs on dark, deserted roads. Tonight, her passenger seat was occupied by her next assignment and an antique dagger with a peculiar handle wedged between the creases of the seat. The folder did not have much information. These assignments never did. All she got was the name, address, time, and place the assignment was carried out. This folder had a picture of a man paper clipped to the cover with the name Kyle Riley written next to it. He was a good-looking man not much older than her; Sabine had wondered about him since she received the documents.

Her phone buzzed for the fifth time since she had set off on the road trip—a picture of Amalia, her new boss, pulsed with each soft buzz. There was no way she could answer the call while she was driving; okay, that was not true, she just did not want to answer the call. As bosses went, she was missing her previous one. Sabine may have disagreed with her last boss and not seen eye to eye on things, but this new boss was a lot worse. She felt she had jumped out of the frying pan only to land in the fires of hell itself.

Sabine's SUV engine hummed softly as she cruised down the highway, looking for the turnoff to take her to her target's house. Her nerves were so tightly wound that she nearly jumped out of her skin when her GPS told her to take the next turn. As she followed the GPS' instructions, she flicked on her high beams and shuddered. The road ahead fell into the inky darkness. The moonlight was blocked from shining onto the road by the army of towering trees that ran along the road edges. The thick forest ran on for miles, climbing up the hills that sprawled in the distance. There were two, maybe three homes she knew of in this area, and they were spread far apart. The house she was heading towards was the remotest of them all. Making it the perfect place to carry out her mission.

Sabine pulled into the driveway, and turning off the lights, she drifted to a safe distance from the house before turning off her car. She sighed, picking up the dagger from the seat, turning it over in her hand. Even in the dark, the strange metal blade and the bejeweled handle had a soft glow. Usually, she used her own tools to carry out a job, but this one had a special request for this blade to be used.

Sabine glanced at the clock. It was almost midnight. Time to complete the contract. She placed the dagger in the sheath on her belt, and then slipped on her long black cloak. She always felt like a cross between a little Red Riding Hood and a dark witch when donning it. Truthfully though, it was more like the Grim Reaper's outfit bringing death to those she encountered when she had it on. If Sabine were a normal person, what she was about to do would be seen as murder, and she would probably be called an assassin. But Sabine was not a normal person, and her job was not that of an assassin; her job was to reap souls.

/ / /

THE FULL MOON hung heavily in the sky, frowning down upon her as she silently crept up the stairs of Kyle Riley's house. At the front door, Sabine waved her hand, and the door quietly clicked open. Slowly, she entered, stepping into the living room illuminated by the moon's silver light, which cast its eerie fingers over the antique furniture and trapping dust particles in the air. The sound of clinking dishes caught her attention, making her turn her head towards the back of the house where Sabine presumed the kitchen would be. The light shining from the doorway confirmed her suspicion that the target or she hoped it was the target, was still awake.

Sabine inched through the doorway of the kitchen, watching Kyle preparing a mug of coffee with his back turned to her. Her fingers slid down the dagger's handle and unsheathed it, holding it in her hand hidden by her cloak as she approached him.

"Kyle Riley, it is time for your soul to move on and take up its next life." Sabine's soft voice carried across the kitchen.

Startled, Kyle swung around; his coffee cup flew out of his hand and crashed to the floor. Before he had time to move or react, Sabine did something she had never done before; she charged at him. The impact of her body flying into him shoved him back against the counter as the deadly blade entered his chest directly into his heart. His stunned eyes turned lifeless before his body landed next to the broken coffee cup.

Sabine removed the dagger from Kyle's chest, her brow creasing as no blood seeped from the wound or clung to the blade. No blue light appeared to open up a portal through the veil to the valley of souls. Confusion turned to shock as she turned around and found Kyle standing behind her, his eyes filled with fear and confusion.

What the hell had just happened? Sabine's mind reeled as she stood staring at the man's soul while his body lay lifeless on the floor by her feet. In all her years, this had never happened to her, nor had she ever heard of it happening or been warned it could happen.

Sabine and Kyle stood staring at each other for a few seconds before the shock wore off, and Kyle lunged for her. His hands left a cold feeling as they sliced through her.

"What the hell have you done to me?" Kyle yelled at her.

Well, he still clearly had a voice. Sabine thought as she watched him flailing about, trying to grab or hit at things, only to find his hand going right through them. He swore blindly as he could not feel nor touch anything he came into contact with. Then he spotted his body lying crumpled on the floor next to Sabine. His eye once again grew large with shock; his head snapped around to glare at her.

"Why am I lying on the floor?" He asked her, "Am I …" he looked back down at his body, closing his ghostly eyes before turning back to her, "I'm dead, aren't I?"

Sabine nodded; she did not know what to say. Usually, the only time she spoke with the dead was when they needed help stepping into the blue light or tried to escape it. She was at a loss for words and was really confused about why the door did not open for him. Sabine looked at his body again; still, there was no blood seeping from the wound.

What was going on? She looked at Kyle, standing there staring at his dead body. Who was he? Or what was he? Had she overlooked something in his file?

"You killed me!" The shock of seeing his dead body started to wear off, and anger took its place. "You bitch! What the bloody hell did I ever do to you?" Kyle began to scream at her. "Have we ever met? Is this some sort of sick vengeance because I rebuffed you at some point? Or did I have a drunken night with you that were so unforgettable that I don't remember you?"

His abusive words spewed out of his ghostly lips while his ghostly form still tried to hit or grab objects around. Sabine stood watching him and listening to his rants while her mind ran through some scenarios as to why this was happening. She glanced up at the clock hanging on the wall; it was almost twenty past twelve, and time was running out. They were going to miss the veil. She needed to think. She needed to figure this out; she could do this, but first, she had to shut him the hell up.

"Can you just shut up for a minute?" Sabine's voice reverberated through the kitchen. She had not meant to shout so loud, but his constant barrage of verbal abuse, mixed with her high-stress levels and this mess, just lit the fuse to a volatile powder keg. "Just keep quiet, please. I need to think."

Surprised by her outburst, Kyle fell instantly silent and stood watching her start to pace around his kitchen. Sabine stopped at his body, looking down at it before turning back to him.

"Blood, where is your blood?" She asked him, making him lean forward to look down at the wound.

"I don't know. Maybe that weird-looking knife you have sucked it all up?" Kyle answered angrily.

Sabine held up the dagger, turning it over before shaking her head, "No, I don't think so." She sheathed the dagger, and then sat down on her haunches to examine the wound. There was no blood even though the flesh was soft and normal. "Have you ever cut yourself and not bled?"

Kyle looked at her as if she was a mad person. "No, I bleed just like every other person on the planet."

"Are you human?" Sabine asked him and watched for his reaction, which was one of surprise, followed once again by the look you give mad people.

"No, I'm Bigfoot, some mythical beast who wanders the forests leaving huge footprints everywhere," he spat at her sarcastically. "Of course, I'm a human who bleeds."

She stood up. Shaking her head, her patience with this man had long since run out. He was rude, abusive, and downright insulting. She was starting to realize why someone thought it time his soul moved on. But he was not lying about being human as there were no signs that he was otherworldly, which meant she was going to have to get help.

Sabine walked out of the kitchen. Reaching into her jeans' pocket for her phone, she rolled her eyes at Amalia's missed calls.

What was up with her? Since Amalia gave her this assignment, she had been on Sabine's back about it, micro-managing her. Ignoring the missed calls, Sabine scrolled through her contacts until she found her aunt's number.

"Sabine, dear," Aunt Lydia's soft, soothing voice answered on the third ring.

"Aunt Lydia, I have a bit of a problem with my latest assignment," Sabine told her aunt. "I have no idea what to do, and I am now left with a dead body and a furious spirit," she whispered into the phone, then went on to tell her aunt what had happened.

"Sabine, you are going to have to bring both the man's body and soul to me," Lydia instructed Sabine. "Do not call anyone else; just get here as quickly as possible."

Sabine stood in the dark lounge for a minute, patting the cell phone against her forehead while she gathered herself to go and face an angry Kyle. That man was a real piece of work. Yes, she had killed him, but to be fair, she had had no idea that there was something strange or cursed about him. And she was more than sure there was nothing in the file mentioning anything about it. It could have been the dagger, but she had wielded other people's daggers before. As long as they had done the sacred ritual that transferred temporary ownership and power, she could wield another person's dagger just as effectively.

Sabine stood at the kitchen door, watching Kyle's spirit standing, staring down at his dead body. He would not like what came next, and worst, she would have to move the body as a normal person did. Their protocol dictated that she could not use any powers in front of or witnessed by a human. He looked like he was quite a solid mass of muscle, and it was going to be a struggle to get him into her SUV.

/ / /

"BE CAREFUL," Kyle shouted as Sabine dragged his body down the stairs.

"I am trying," Sabine shouted back at him as she walked backwards down the stairs. Her arms were hooked under his armpits as she dragged his legs and feet across the ground.

"My goodness, you are heavy!" Sabine moaned after opening the trunk of the SUV and hefting his body into it. "If you want answers, I suggest you get into the car as well," she commanded his ghostly form.

Kyle stood staring at the door and then at her before saying, "Are you going to open it for me or what?"

Sabine deliberately walked to the driver's side and yanked open the door. She was getting so tired of his rudeness. "In case you have not noticed, you are a ghost, so move through the door." She jumped into the driver's seat, slamming the door shut and starting the engine as Kyle morphed through the passenger door.

"If I was not so pissed off and dead, that would have been quite cool," he said, and then swore when he realized he could not use the safety belt.

"Dead, remember?" Sabine told him sarcastically. "So, you don't need the seat belt." She removed her cape and tossed it onto the back seat, not missing the stunned look on Kyle's face as her form came back into shape.

"What?" she asked him as he sat there gaping at her.

"You are a lot younger than I imagined you would be beneath your Grim Reaper ninja outfit." He frowned, looking at her jeans, sneakers, and a soft pink t-shirt. Sabine could almost feel what he was thinking. "And you look just like a normal person."

"What were you expecting?" she asked him as she started the car and backed out of the driveway.

"I don't know. Warts and a long, hooked nose?" Kyle swore as she drove off with squealing tires, and he could not grab onto anything. "If you keep driving like this, you won't need a seat belt soon, either," he sneered.

TWO

A Cursed Soul

"WHAT IS THIS PLACE, A HUNTING CABIN?" KYLE ASKED, making a face as he looked at the rustic log cabin that looked like it had been built during the Wild West.

"It is my aunt's home," Sabine told him and felt annoyed as she slammed out of the truck, leaving him to exit through the passenger side door. "My aunt is going to try and help you." She pointed her finger at his chest, only to hit the air as it went right through him.

"How many wind chimes can one person have," Kyle tried to push one of the many, many weird-shaped wind chimes hanging around the patio that surrounded the cabin. "You do know if anyone comes at you with an ax out here, you are on your own?" He looked around the heavily wooded area that was even more remote than his house was. "Creepy." Kyle gave an exaggerated shudder as he looked at what appeared to be a tiny skull and some bones on a table next to which an old rocking chair sat.

Sabine glanced at her watch; it was one-thirty in the morning, but she knew her aunt was awake as she reached out to knock on the door. She hoped her aunt could help with this situation because this man was starting to drive her crazy.

The door swung open, and her aunt greeted Sabine with a hug as she stepped over the threshold. However, when Kyle tried to enter the house, he found that he could not.

"You must be the lost soul," Lydia watched Kyle repeatedly try to enter her house. "You may as well stop trying because the likes of you and anything else that is not welcome, cannot cross the threshold."

"I will just wait out here then," Kyle said sarcastically. "I can't feel the cold anyway, and as I am dead, not much can harm me," he ended with a yell.

"Cantankerous guy, isn't he?" Lydia turned back towards her niece, ignoring Kyle grumbling just outside of her front door.

"Just close the door, and then we won't be able to hear him," Sabine grinned at the look Kyle gave her. "I have not had a quiet moment since I met him."

"You mean murdered me." Kyle corrected her.

"I did not murder you!" Sabine put her hands on her hips. "It was your time to move on for whatever reason the powers that be had."

"Why would the powers that be, whoever they are, want me dead?" Kyle yelled.

"After spending this past hour or so with you, I can understand why they would want you to move on," Sabine yelled back.

"Okay, you two calm down," Lydia intervened, not liking her peace disrupted by yelling and negativity.

"The man is impossible," Sabine was clearly exasperated.

"Well, honey, his life has just ended, and for some reason, he is stuck here, like that." Lydia gestured towards

Kyle's form. "He has every reason to be upset and confused."

Sabine watched Kyle exploring Lydia's long wind chimes that hung near the door. They were magical chimes that could change shape and form if you asked them things or touched them, and they could pick up on mood vibrations. Right now, they were pulsing red from the heated argument Sabine and Kyle were having.

"Where is his body?" Lydia asked Sabine.

"In the trunk of my car," Sabine answered as she and Lydia stepped around Kyle's ghostly form to go to the SUV.

Sabine popped open the trunk to reveal Kyle's body covered by a tarp. She yanked back the tarp and swallowed, shuddering; the body had started to decompose. Soon rigor mortis would set in, and she noted that it had already begun in the jaw and neck. His skin had gone a yellowish color from the loss of blood circulation. His body was becoming a bit swollen from the leaking enzymes that cause gas to build up in it. Sabine did not like being around dead bodies. She usually never had to be; that is what the cleanup crew was for. It was only this time she could not get them involved until Kyle's soul moved on.

"Look what you've done to me," Kyle hissed, looking over their shoulders at his body.

"Help me with this," Lydia asked Sabine as she started to look over Kyle's body, starting with his arms that were visible in his short-sleeved shirt.

Sabine helped her aunt maneuver the body that felt a bit spongy, making Sabine cringe as she touched it. "Gross," Sabine winced as his fingers accidentally squeezed his arm too tight.

"Hey, watch it." Kyle grouched at her, receiving a deep sigh and rolled eyes from Sabine.

"We have to remove his clothes." Lydia started to unbutton Kyle's shirt, which he was not at all happy about.

"I don't think so, lady." Kyle tried to cover his body with his ghostly form, only to have the two women ignore him. "I am warning you …" he yelled as Lydia thoroughly examined his well-defined torso. "What are you looking for?"

"Shut up," Sabine yelled at Kyle. They were trying to concentrate and do a thorough examination in light that was not that good. His constant nagging, moaning, screaming, and snide remarks were doing her head in. "I want this over as much as you do. I probably want it to be over more than you do! So, just float … or whatever it is you do away and let us finish."

Kyle stared at Sabine in shock; he did not expect her to erupt like that. Sabine glared back at him. She stood her ground, refusing to let her guilt at what happened to him make her go soft. Her nerves were frayed enough as it was doing this job nearly every day; she had not needed this to happen.

"How would you like someone poking around your body, and all you could do was watch?" Kyle said a bit more calmly.

"Look, I know this must be confusing and stressful for you." Sabine tried to search for the words to say to him. "I do not know why you were targeted or why your soul would not cross the veil." Sabine chewed her nails as she pondered on their predicament. "But, I promise you, we are going to find out. Okay?"

Kyle nodded; stepping out of the way so Sabine and Lydia could carry on looking for whatever it was they were looking for on his corpse.

"Thank you," Sabine told him softly before leaning in to help her aunt resume the inspection. "What is this?"

Sabine asked her aunt, pointing to a weird mark that resembled a symbol on Kyle's lower back.

"Let me see," Lydia shone her phone light onto the mark. "I see ..." Lydia ran her fingers over the mark before examining it closer.

Lydia did not say another word. She respectfully nested Kyle's clothes and positioned his body in a more peaceful pose before covering it with the tarp. Lydia turned and walked towards the porch where Kyle had retreated to. She made herself comfortable in one of her rocking chairs, indicating that Kyle and Sabine did the same.

"Now Kyle, I need to know if anything strange has happened to you within the past week or two." Sabine noted her aunt watching Kyle closely.

"No, not that I can think of." Kyle frowned at Lydia.

"There is a mark," Lydia told him. "It is an unusual looking scratch on your lower back." Lydia leaned forward, pointing to the same position on her back. "I see that it may have felt like it was infected."

"Yes, I know the mark. It burned and itched a lot," Kyle told her, "I have been putting various salves on it, but it does not seem to want to heal. Wait ..." Kyle looked at Lydia, his brow creased. "You don't think that mark is why I am like this?"

"It is no ordinary mark, Kyle," Sabine informed him. "In fact, it looks like an ancient symbol of sorts." Sabine nibbled on her nails and bounced her knee while her mind raced to try to think why that symbol looked so familiar to her.

"Yes, you are correct, my dear," Lydia confirmed what Sabine had said. "It is part of a ritual that, as far as I know, has not been practiced for centuries."

"What are you talking about?" Kyle looked at the two women as if they each had three heads. "I scratched myself about ten days ago when I went to the city to meet someone."

"Would that someone happen to have been a female?" Lydia asked Kyle.

"Yes, but what does that have to do with anything. And I am pretty sure she did not perform any rituals while carving a mark on me," Kyle sputtered angrily. He did not like people prying into his private affairs.

"The woman you went to meet. Did you know her well?" Lydia asked him as she gently stopped Sabine from chewing off her nails down to the nail beds.

"I don't see how any of that is relevant to my current situation!" Kyle huffed, not comfortable with this line of questioning. "We met up for dinner and drinks in the city."

"Did the two of you have sex during the meet up?" Lydia asked him calmly, ignoring Kyle's anger and discomfort.

"I do not have to sit here and be grilled about my sex life with you." Kyle stood up and pushed the chair back. Only the chair did not move, and Kyle found himself standing in the middle of the chair as he went right through it.

"Kyle, my aunt is not interested in your sex life. We are trying to figure out if this woman at any time came into close contact with your body," Sabine explained to him. "That mark you have on your body is not just a scratch as you presumed it was."

"Is she the last person you came into close contact with in the past ten days?" Lydia asked him.

"Yes, she is the only person I have had close contact with in the past ten days," Kyle sighed. "And yes, we had sex after dinner if you must know."

"Was there anything a bit peculiar about the woman or the sex?" Lydia asked unabashedly.

"Do you want a play by play? Maybe record it, so you have some kinky ritual sex tape?" Kyle spat angrily, before folding his arm defensively.

"Kyle, we need to know if you at any time thought there was anything strange about the woman or the intimacy," Sabine's voice was soft and soothing. The type of voice one used to get a child to open up.

Kyle looked at her, and their eyes held. Sabine gave him an encouraging smile.

"No, there was nothing unusual about her, or anything else," he looked away. Sabine and her aunt exchanged a glance. He was not telling them the truth.

"Do you at least have a name for us?" Lydia asked him.

"Elissa, she did not give me her last name," Kyle turned and wandered off the porch's far side.

"What are you thinking, aunty?" Sabine knew that look on her aunt's face; it usually never ended with anything good.

"Kyle has been cursed." Lydia leaned forward and picked up a strange black crystal from the table in front of her. She started to gently rub it with her fingers, warming the stone before handing it to her niece. "You need to keep this Jet stone with you." Lydia put the stone into the palm of Sabine's hand. "It will keep you safe from the curse."

"Curse?" Kyle shot back to where Lydia and Sabine were. He could move fast now that he did not have any flesh to restrict his movement.

"I'm afraid so, Kyle," Lydia told him calmly. "It is a rather nasty curse, one I have not seen in a very long time."

"Okay, wait just a minute." Kyle held up his hand as if he was warning someone to stop. "You are telling me that I am the way I am now because of a curse?" He shook his head, "A voodoo, hoodoo, mumbo jumbo, bibbity bobbity boop type curse?"

"No, more like something dark and ancient," Lydia told him frankly.

"Are you being serious?" Kyle could still not believe what he was hearing, although nothing should surprise him as he was now a ghost.

"Very," Lydia stood up. "This particular curse leaves you damned to walk the earth in a ghostly form for eternity as it stops your soul from moving on to the afterlife."

"What!" Kyle stood there, staring at Lydia in shock. This indeed was a night from hell.

"Aunty, is there any way the curse can be lifted?" Sabine, who had been quietly watching the conversation between her aunt and Kyle, asked. "Do you know of any rituals we may perform or something we can do?" Sabine's eyes were huge and tormented. "I either need to complete this job or somehow return Kyle to his body before it is too late."

"You can return me to my body?" Kyle appeared in front of her.

"No," Lydia said vehemently. "That will not be possible as your body has already started to decay." Lydia shuddered, thinking about the consequences of returning a freed soul to its flesh form. "Unless you want to walk the earth with both a cursed body and soul." Lydia's voice held a warning, and her eyes flashed with an emotion Sabine could not quite pinpoint.

"Aunty, what do you mean? The body has not even been buried." Sabine's voice sounded hopeful. "Surely, if we can lift the curse, we will be able to …"

Lydia cut Sabine's words off. "No, Sabine. Do not even entertain that idea. That is not a price neither you nor he would want to pay." Lydia turned to walk back inside, and stopping just over the threshold, she closed her eyes and chanted a few words.

Lydia opened her eyes. Picking up a small bowl from the table next to the door, she sprinkled a fine powder over the door frame. "Now, we need to bring Kyle's body to the altar room. I need to perform a cleansing so his body will be welcomed back into the earth to give him peace."

"Why is she keeping my body?" Kyle asked as he followed Sabine down the stairs back to the car. "We need to keep my body close to us." He whispered.

"Sure, that is a great idea," Sabine told him sarcastically as she opened the trunk and waited for her aunt. "Drive around with a dead, decaying body in my car that will rot even quicker as the temperatures are going to be around seventy-eight to eighty degrees today."

"Okay, sorry for not wanting to let go of my body!" Kyle scathed at her.

Sabine sighed and then completely ignored him again as he was grumbling about how she and her aunt were handling him. Never mind that both Sabine and her aunt were of a small framed stature while Kyle was a six-foot block of muscle.

"I HOPE that is the last time I have to lug your body up and downstairs," Sabine grumbled, pulling out of her aunt's driveway and heading towards the city. Her arms felt bruised from all the heavy lifting she had done in the last couple of hours.

"If you had not killed me in the first place, you would not have had to drag me anywhere." Kyle gave her a tight smile.

"Look, I am not ..." Sabine was interrupted by her

phone; it was Amalia. Drat! Sabine thought she would have to answer it and let her boss know what was going on.

Sabine indicated for Kyle to be quiet as she put her wireless earpiece into her ear and answered the call.

"Sabine, why have you been avoiding my calls?" Amalia's voice echoed through the earpiece. Even when she was angry, her voice sounded sultry, like she was purring. "I have been trying to reach you for hours."

"Sorry, Amalia, but I have been a bit busy taking care of the assignment," Sabine answered truthfully, not realizing she was once again chewing on her nails. "There has been a bit of a problem," Sabine explained the situation to Amalia.

"Well, that certainly is a dilemma, Sabine, one I am sure you are going to fix right away as your target needs to die." Amalia hissed vehemently, making Sabine frown.

"I am working on it," Sabine promised to keep Amalia updated on the situation before hanging up. She was puzzled as to why Amalia was taking such a personal interest in this case.

"Who was that?" Kyle was not very happy with having overheard a conversation about his death and feeling a little overwhelmed that someone wanted him dead.

"My boss," Sabine told him as she took the earpiece out of her ear and made sure it was turned off. "She usually does not take such an interest in these cases." Sabine's brows creased for a second before she turned her attention back to the task at hand.

THREE

An Expensive Date

SABINE AND KYLE SAT IN HER SUV ACROSS FROM THE restaurant Kyle had met Elissa at. Kyle had not been too forthcoming with the information about Elissa. All Sabine could get from him on the drive into the city was that they had met at the restaurant. He did not even have her last name. He had swiped right, and so had she on some hook-up phone app. Sabine used her phone as little as possible, and in her line of work, social media was not advisable. Dating or hook-up apps were not her thing. In fact, Sabine could not remember the last time she had gone on a date.

"So, now it's your turn to tell me something about yourself," Kyle noted the dashboard's time. "We have some time to kill before the restaurant opens for breakfast. I have answered many of your questions; now it is my turn to get some answers." He gave Sabine a genuine smile, which nearly took her breath away.

He was a handsome man in a rugged sort of way. Sabine thought before giving herself a mental slap in the face. "Okay, I guess that is fair." She took off her seat belt and made herself more comfortable on the seat. "What do you want to know?"

"Tell me about your job." Kyle frowned, "I mean, who steals people's souls for a living?"

"I do not steal people's souls." Sabine defended, "There are times when souls need to move on as it is their time. If they do not move on, it can have a ripple effect through time."

"On time?" Kyle looked at her skeptically, "So, what if you have someone who can see the future and they say, oh he is going to cause World War Three, best we get rid of him now?"

"No, that is not how it works." Sabine started to chew on her thumbnail, "There is a lot about this world that humans are completely oblivious to. Those that do have an inkling are usually labeled as crazy; most humans cannot handle the truth, so it does drive them crazy." Sabine glanced at the restaurant. Someone was unlocking the door.

"So, those are the people's souls you reap?" Kyle asked her. "People who have found out about your strange world?"

"No, not at all," Sabine shook her head. "Actually, I don't ever get given the reason for the reaping," she said quietly.

He had hit upon one of the things that always bothered Sabine. One of the reasons she never wanted to join the family business. She was never allowed to ask why the person's soul needed to move on. She could understand those who were dying, in excruciating pain, and even a few people with dark souls. But most of the souls she reaped lately were still healthy and good people as far as she could tell. And Sabine was very sensitive to people, a gift she hid from everyone, especially her family. Things did not end well for Empaths in her family, so she kept that ability to herself.

"When a soul has to move on, they have to move on, and trust me, it is better that I help them cross-over rather than the alternative."

Sabine gave a little shudder as she thought of the dark reapers in the world. They were an ancient race of which thankfully there were not many, if any, left in this world.

"So, then you have no idea why you were sent to reap my soul?" Kyle asked her, his brows drawn together as he stared at her in disbelief. "You just came hurtling at me with your soul-sucking knife with no clue as to why you were to take my soul?" He was getting angry again.

"I …" Sabine closed her mouth. She did not know what to say to that. He was right. "Look, I am going to do everything I can to fix this."

Even though he was just a soul, Sabine could feel his distress emanating from him, and it sliced through her. She swallowed and breathed to center herself so she could switch off her feelings.

This was not the time to allow any in as she had a job to finish. "I promise you, we are going to find out what is going on, and I will do whatever I can to fix this."

"And then what?" Kyle asked her, anger boiling through his soul, "Are you going to somehow stuff my soul back into my rotting corpse." He yelled at her, but before she could answer, the restaurant opened.

Saved by the bell! Literally, the bell indicating the restaurant was opened rang a few times. One of the oldest churches in the city had been converted into the restaurant they were waiting to go into. The area they were in was where the original town had started hundreds of years ago before it sprawled into its city. The restaurant had kept the church look and the large brass bell in the bell tower that topped it. Every time the restaurant opened or closed, they would ring the bell. It was also rung to indicate when they were serving lunch or dinner menus. The charm of the restaurant and its excellent food was what made the Old Church Restaurant such a popular one.

"How did you get a reservation here?" Sabine asked Kyle, who had once again fallen into a bad mood. "This place is booked up months in advance for breakfast, lunch, and supper."

"I have my connections," Kyle told her, shrugging and not saying anymore on the subject as they got to the restaurant door.

Before Sabine could open the door, it was opened for her by a well-dressed server. "Good morning." The man greeted Sabine with a huge smile.

"Good morning to you too," Sabine smiled back at the man.

"May I have the name your reservation is under?" he asked her kindly.

"I don't have one," Sabine told the man, watching his brows lift in surprise. Before he could say to her it was reservations only, she said, "I am here because I am a private investigator. I just need some information on one of your patrons."

"I am sorry, but I am not allowed to give out details about our patrons," the man said with feigned regret.

"Oh, no, I don't want information about them. I just need to know if any of the staff here remember seeing ..." Sabine handed the man the picture of Kyle she had taken from his folder, "This man here about ten nights ago?"

"I can tell you that we all remember that man," the man's eyes narrowed on Sabine. "Why are you asking about him?"

"I am trying to track down the person he was with on that night," she told the man.

"Well, I can tell you she was blonde, beautiful, with the most startling blue eyes. I think every red-blooded man, no matter his sexual orientation, was drawn to her," the man sighed and then shivered as Kyle went behind him. Then through him, to get a look at the booking register. "Sorry, there seems to be a very chilly breeze in here." The man looked around for the source of the cold.

"Is there anything else you could tell me about her or him?" Sabine asked the man, trying to ignore Kyle, who was now enjoying himself, making the poor man shiver.

"Yes," he said, rather animatedly. "She wore the most gorgeous green gem necklace." He touched his neck as he thought about it. "Oh, and we had to kick them both out as he, he…" pointing to Kyle's picture, "caused a drunken scene."

"Well, thank you for your time." Sabine handed him one of her cards, "If you think of anything else about them or that night that seemed unusual, please call me."

"I will," the man called after her as she left, taking the source of the man's cold breeze with her.

/ / /

"WELL, that was a giant waste of time," Kyle said as he drifted through the car door and onto the passenger seat.

"No, it was quite informative," Sabine leaned forward over the steering wheel, thinking. Something about the way he described the woman and her necklace seemed so familiar to Sabine as a memory nag at the back of her mind just out of reach.

"How is that guy telling you he had to kick me out because I was drunk helpful?" Kyle huffed. He was still angry about the previous conversation. "How dare he? If I was not in the shape I am in, I would have demanded he get fired." Kyle crossed his ghostly arms, sitting back angrily and nearly falling right through the seat.

"Were you?" Sabine asked him distractedly as she took out her phone to call her aunt. Maybe Lydia would also recognize the woman's description.

"Was I what?" Kyle asked impatiently.

"Drunk and being rude to the staff?" Sabine looked at him with her phone to her ear. Her aunt did not answer, and the phone went to voicemail. That was strange! Sabine thought; her aunt always answered her phone no matter what time of the day or night it was, especially if she heard that it was the ring tone indicating the call was from Sabine.

"I most certainly was …" Kyle's voice trailed off as he noted the look of worry on Sabine's face. "Is something wrong?"

"My aunt." After trying her aunt's phone for the third time, Sabine said, "She is not answering her phone."

"Maybe she did not hear it, or she is in the shower." Kyle tried to ease her mind. He could see she was quite stricken for some reason.

"No, she would have answered." Sabine had the most dreadful feeling and knew that it had something to do with that green gem necklace without a shadow of a doubt. "We have to get back to my aunt's house," Sabine said as an overwhelming feeling of panic flooded her.

///

THE MINUTE they drove into Lydia's drive, Sabine knew that she was right. There was something wrong with her aunt. Without waiting for Kyle or offering an explanation,

Sabine flew out of the car, dashing inside her aunt's house.

"Aunt Lydia," Sabine called as she dialed her aunt's mobile phone.

Sabine stood silent for a minute listening; she could hear the ring coming from the kitchen. The phone was there but not her aunt. Not finding her aunt in the house, Sabine went down to the altar room in the small church-like building that adorned the house's back. It was here in the altar room where Sabine saw and felt signs of a struggle. She also noticed that Kyle's body was no longer there.

Walking through the kitchen, Sabine found a dagger, nearly the exact same as the one she had been given to reap Kyle's soul, laying on the floor. Only this dagger had a red gem in it and not an amber one like the one she had used on Kyle had. Again, that irksome memory about the green jewel refused to come out and show itself. Frustrated, Sabine stormed out of the house, nearly walking right through Kyle, who was stuck at her aunt's threshold.

"Is everything okay?" He asked her, his eyes dropping to the dagger in her hand, "Why did you take your dagger with you?"

"It is not my dagger. I found it on the kitchen floor," she held the dagger up to look at it. The dagger's design and patterns mimicked the one in her car; it also had that warm feeling and felt like it was pulsing. It was almost as if the dagger was alive; as the thought flashed across her mind, a feeling of great pain stabbed through her. Sabine gasped and dropped the knife, grabbing her throat and the door frame to steady herself.

"Sabine," Kyle tried to reach out to her only to be blasted back by the protection field.

"I'm fine." Sabine coughed, and drawing in a ragged breath, she steadied herself. The first time she had touched the other dagger; she had remembered getting a weird vibe from it. She had thrown it on the seat because of the feeling that had shot through her. "My aunt is gone, and so is your body."

Sabine leaned down and picked up the knife, ignoring Kyle as he swore up a storm. Ignoring the heat from the dagger pulsing in her hand, Sabine walked back to her car, tossing the dagger into the glove compartment.

"If we find out whose dagger it is, I am sure we will find both my aunt and your body." Sabine put her seat belt on; the hand in which she had held the dagger tingled like she had been shocked by an electric socket. "Kyle," Sabine looked at him, a serious expression on her face, "Is there anything you are keeping from me about Elissa and the night you met her?"

"Not this again." Kyle disappeared out of the car.

Sabine was sure if he could have, he would have slammed out of the car in a huff. She now knew without a shadow of a doubt there was something he was not telling her about Elissa. That angered her as now her aunt was missing too; any information that he had could help Sabine find Lydia and maybe even save him. She released her seatbelt and jumped out of the car, storming after him.

"Look, you have every right to be angry at me. I under-stand that." Sabine's cheeks flamed while her eyes flashed angrily, "But my aunt has only been trying to help you, and now she has gone missing for her efforts." She took a deep breath pursing her lips as she ran her hands over her face in frustration. This whole job was a nightmare, and she was sure she had an ulcer now.

"I am sorry about your aunt," Kyle looked at her, his anger making his eyes slit. "But you know, I was just getting ready to go and check the traps out in the woods," he advanced towards her. "Only this crazy person in a black cape drew a dagger and killed me," he yelled at her. "Now apparently, I am cursed to roam the Earth as a cursed soul because I had a night out with a beautiful woman."

"So, it's my fault you troll dating apps looking for one night stands with beautiful women because you don't know how to have a real relationship?" Sabine yelled back at him. She had had about enough of his pity party and guilt-trip he kept laying on her. "Just get in the freakin' truck if you want me to try and save your sorry ass." She turned and sauntered off to her SUV, yanking the driver's door open and hoisting herself in.

Sabine started her car, too upset to care if Kyle was in it or not. As she began to back up, Kyle popped into the passenger seat.

They glared at each for a second. "I hope whoever Elissa was that she was worth it. Because she is probably the most expensive and last date of your life," Sabine pointed out to him, before turning her attention to the road.

The car fell silent on the drive back to the city, giving Sabine time to formulate a plan to find her aunt and possibly save Kyle. Their first stop was her office. She needed to find the owner of the knives she now had in her possession. She was also going to break protocol and find out precisely why Kyle had been targeted. Sabine glanced at him; her heart did a weird jolt as she felt oddly drawn to him.

"I promise I will do everything I can to save you," Sabine promised him quietly. Their eyes met, and he gave her a sad smile. His hand reaching over to cup hers, only, it went straight through.

"I know we will find your aunt," Kyle told her softly and fell into silence for the rest of the city's journey.

FOUR

A House Full of Surprises

Sabine brought the car to a stop in front of a two-story house that looked like all the other houses on the block.

"I thought we were going to your office." Kyle looked around the neighborhood, "Are we making a pit stop at your place?" He gave her a teasing smile and enjoyed the way her cheeks flamed.

"No, this is the office." She unbuckled her seat belt before reaching over him to grab the folder and knife allocated to her for the contract. "It is designed to not draw attention to our kind or the organization."

"It does look just like the other one." Kyle eyed the weapon that Sabine had stabbed him with.

"Yes, it is almost identical except for the jewel." Sabine made sure not to touch the red jeweled dagger and left it in the glove compartment. She would make sure she had her cape on before attempting to touch it again.

"You said that they were not your knives?" Kyle asked her curiously.

"No, the one with the amber jewel on it was given to

me to use for this assignment," she looked at him, smiling apologetically. "I'm sorry, that must have sounded cold."

"It's okay; I'm getting used to all this weird stuff." Kyle gave her a small laugh.

"I have my own dagger, left to me by my mother," Sabine smiled sadly, looking down at the folder with Kyle's name on it. "I come from a long line of reapers." Sabine shook her head, "I tried so hard not to get drawn into this," she said softly, swallowing the lump rising in her throat. "A couple of months ago, I was an advertising executive." She laughed at the shocked look on Kyle's face.

"Well, I guess it is not that much of a career change," Kyle's jest made her laugh, breaking the car's tension. "So, how does this work then?"

"What?" Sabine looked at him, confused for a minute before realizing he was talking about the contracts.

"The contracts," Kyle asked her, "Do you just get given the name, and then told to go forth and reap?"

"It is not that simple, and right now, I do not have the time to explain it. The people in the house can sense I am here. They will also be able to sense you, so you will need to put…" Sabine leaned over and grabbed her black cloak off the back seat, "this over you."

"First, that is a woman's clothing item," Kyle recoiled in horror. "Second, I'm a ghost, it is going to …" before he could finish, Sabine waved her hands, and the cloak surrounded him. "Never mind then."

"We do not have long as this spell only lasts for ninety minutes if we are lucky." Sabine climbed out of the car. "Don't try to speak or touch anything. You may look like you have a body, but you are pretty much still a ghost. The cloak is what you would call a smokescreen."

"Cool, like a human suit for a ghost?" He gave her a cheeky lopsided grin.

Sabine wanted to laugh; he had no idea that the cloak made him look like the actual Grim Reaper. She played with the idea of giving him a scythe but thought it was best not to push their luck.

///

"OH," Sabine stopped at the door, "Don't speak; let me do all the talking." He nodded, wishing he had hands to swat hers away as she fiddled with the cape.

"Sabine, it is good to see you." The concierge ducked down to greet them. He looked a bit like Frankenstein's monster, only without the green color and sewn-up look. He was also very, very tall, having to duck to clear a six-foot-five door frame.

"Hello Robert, it is always good to see you." Sabine hugged the gentle giant, "This is one of the reapers doing their rounds with me."

"Of course, any reaper with you is one we welcome here." Robert bowed and allowed them both entrance into the house. He walked with them to the back of the house, where he opened another door for them. The door led to some stairs that went down into a well-lit basement. An enormous basement that housed an underworld of offices that looked like any other office block.

"Wow." Kyle whistled softly, "This is cool." He looked around the underground network in amazement.

"It can get a bit too much if you have to work here for eight to ten hours a day. That is why the office staff only work three days a week and get two outside breaks a day, plus lunchtime, of course."

"That seems fair." Kyle looked around at the people working there, wondering if they were all reapers and, if not, what types of magical being they were. "Is everyone here a witch or warlock type person?"

"No, and it is offensive to call anyone who is part of our way of life a witch or warlock." Sabine joked with him. "They prefer to be called magical beings."

"Ahh, okay," Kyle shook his head, smiling to himself. He bet magical beings were one group you did not want to offend. You could end up like a toad or a ghost. He looked down at the magic cloak he was wearing to cloak his cursed soul.

"We need to go to the library. There is someone there who will know whose knives these are." Sabine gripped the folder, "It's this way." She turned down another corridor that ended with a large wooden door.

"What happened to you when you touched the knife with the red jewel in it?" Kyle's questions made Sabine stop so suddenly, he nearly bumped into her.

"You cannot tell anyone about that," Sabine whispered to him, turning around abruptly, not realizing how close he was. The cloak brushed against her, giving her a warm tingling feeling as if Kyle himself had touched her.

"I, uh …" She cleared her throat and took a step back, bumping into the library door. "It was nothing," she said a bit too quickly, and then turned to open the library door, putting her finger on her lips to indicate he needed to keep quiet. A sign hung over the station where the librarian sat that warned all who entered not to raise their voices, eat food, or chew gum in the library. Sabine walked through the library to the room at the back with a sign on the door: Marina Hopkins, Head Librarian.

"Who is Marina?" Kyle whispered as they walked through the library that looked much like any other library did.

"She is the historian with the resources and knowledge

to help us," Sabine walked to another wooden door, gave a soft knock, and waited until they heard "come."

"Hello, Sabine," Marina smiled warmly at her. "What brings you here today?" Marina leaned her head sideways to see who was with Sabine.

"Hello, Marina," Sabine greeted the small petite woman sitting behind her sizeable antique desk. "I need to know who a soul dagger belongs to," She placed the folder on the desk in front of Marina.

"A contract reaping?" Marina's brows creased, "I still feel the company should not allow that practice." She opened the folder and put on a normal-looking rounded pair of glasses.

Marina looked at the dagger, and she was careful not to touch it, before saying, "This dagger belongs to Amalia."

"Are you sure?" Sabine asked Marina in shocked disbelief.

"One hundred percent sure," Marina told Sabine confidently, eyeing her over her glasses' rim.

"Why would Amalia put a contract on a soul?" Sabine lifted her thumb to her mouth, nibbling on her nail.

"That you will have to ask her," Marina said apologetically.

"Have you seen a mark like this before?" Sabine asked Marina, showing her a photo of the mark on Kyle's back.

"I think so," Marina walked over to a section of antique leather-bound books with weird writing on their spines.

She took one out; it was large and heavy, making a thud when Marina dropped it onto the desk. She asked Sabine to run the dagger over the cover. As Sabine did so, the book opened on its own, pages flipping until it stopped on a section.

"That is weird." Marina looked troubled, "The page is missing."

Sabine leaned over, her heart slamming into her ribcage as she recognized the book. "That's my mother's book," she said softly, swallowing down the lump that always formed when her parents' memories haunted her.

"I am so sorry, Sabine." Marina's face fell, "How insensitive of me; yes, it was your mother's. Lydia donated it to the library a few months ago," she told Sabine. "Hayden was the foremost authority on ancient rites and rituals from the light and dark sects." Marina went on to explain, "Her work was invaluable to us all." Marina's eyes filled with tears at the thought of her lifelong best friend.

"It's okay, Marina. I had no use for the books and cannot read that script anyway." Sabine told her, "They are far more useful with you. I know she would have wanted you to have them."

"Thank you, Sabine." Marina sniffed, "But this is worrying that the page is missing."

"What do you mean missing; it looks like it is there." Sabine craned her neck to look at the book.

"No, it goes from page seventy to eighty-three, so thirteen pages are missing."

"But there are no obvious signs that the pages have been torn out of the book."

"That is because you cannot tear them out of the book." Marina pointed her ring that looked like an eye on the book. The lids opened, and the eye color changed to blue, making a mark appear on the page. "See that magic mark on the corner of the page?"

"Yes," Sabine leaned over, trying to avoid the all-seeing eye-ring. She hated those things. They creeped her out.

Her mother used to have one, and so did aunt Lydia; only the high council's matriarchs and high priestesses had them. Marina was awarded hers because she was the keeper of knowledge and seeker of truths. No one chose an all-seeing eye; the eyes would decide who would possess them, or who they would work for. Sabine suppressed a shudder at the thought of those creepy, weird eyes that had been the thing of her nightmares since she was a child.

"Only the one who cast it can remove that mark or a page from this book." Marina frowned, "Which means that it has been enchanted."

"Why would someone enchant thirteen pages of a book?" Sabine looked at Marina, "And what exactly is that book?"

"It's a book on the ancient dark arts," Marina told her. "If I'm not mistaken, the pages that have been spelled are about the dark reapers and the daggers of the doomed."

"The daggers of the doomed?" An image flashed in Sabine's mind, a memory, or a nightmare she once had. She was not quite sure, but a door opened in her mind, and before Sabine could stop herself, she stepped through it.

///

SABINE COULD HEAR her father shouting for her. She was nine years old and playing in her tree house her father had built her in the huge old oak tree that protected their house. Her dad was home! Sabine ran out onto the wooden landing, excited to see him, only it was not her dad who greeted her.

A dark cloud-like shadow descended to the tree house level and started to take on a black ghostly form. Fear gripped her heart, but she could not move, she could not run, she could not scream; she was paralyzed. The figure moved closer to Sabine, her heart pounded in her chest, and her breathing was labored with fear. Something glinted within the cloud, and as The Darkness drew nearer, Sabine could make out an oddly shaped stone. If it didn't have a strange glow, she would not have seen it. As Sabine stared at the glowing gem, her fear subsided, replaced by a deep fascination and need to reach out and touch the gemstone. Her hand seemed to rise on its own accord, reaching through the cold swirling blackness.

Before Sabine could touch the jewel, strong arms surrounded her waist, and she was spun around and dumped inside the tree house. Stunned, she stood staring as her father grabbed the tree house door, pulling it shut. She could hear her mother's screams now and some words being chanted by her father in a language she did not understand. There was a terrible high-pitched noise like a creature being tortured; the tree house shook. Sabine nearly lost her footing as the huge oak groaned and swayed. Still, she instinctively moved with it in a daze, raising her hands to cover her ears as the noise got louder.

Suddenly, the tree stopped swaying, and the world around her went quiet, not a peaceful quiet but that one just before a deadly storm. Sabine's fear started to bubble up in her chest again as she stood staring at the tree house door.

Where were her dad and mom? Why could she not hear them anymore? Was The Darkness still out there?

The door to the tree house flew open, and Sabine screamed, "Mommy, Daddy."

//

"SABINE," Marina shook Sabine again, looking nervously towards the library door, "Sabine, snap out of it." Marina rushed behind her desk and took a sleeping all-seeing eye out of a drawer's pewter box. This eye was on a long silver chain. Marina said a soft incantation before putting it around Sabine's neck. The sleeping eye blinked a few times before opening.

"Eye, do your thing; you know what to do," Marina whispered to it.

The eye blinked. As the color changed to blue, Sabine screamed out for her mom and dad before jolting as she had awakened from a bad dream.

"You. Ghostly man," Marina pointed to Kyle, standing there staring at Sabine in shock. She had said something about daggers, then fell into some sort of a trance.

"Kyle!" Marina shouted at him now.

"You can see me?" He asked the petite woman.

"Of course, I can see you. Who do you think fashioned that cape for Sabine?" Marina told impatiently. "We do not have much time." Marina went over to him and took off the cape, throwing it over Sabine to cover her from head to toe.

"Hey, Sabine said I needed to keep covered in that," Kyle hissed at Marina, feeling exposed and …

Kyle held up his hand; it was flesh again. He patted his face. It was there. He moved to the mirror hanging on the wall, and there he was.

"Am I whole again?" he turned to Marina in amazement, "Did you save me somehow?"

"No and no," Marina was pouring what appeared to be salt around Sabine just as books and other objects in the room started flying everywhere.

"Whoa," Kyle ducked, as a huge book headed straight towards his head, only to be whacked by a chair. "Dang it," he groaned. Yup, he could feel again.

"Don't get too used to it. You can only corporealize for a maximum of twenty to thirty minutes at a time," Marina told him. "Now get over here. I need you to help me calm Sabine down."

"Is she doing all this?" Kyle ducked and dodged a few more items flying at him as he made his way to Marina.

"Yes," Marina confirmed. "It seems you are being targeted." Marina laughed as another item went hurtling at Kyle. "You must have upset her."

"Well ..." Kyle ducked again. "Let's just do this before I lose an eye that I only have for the next few minutes. I don't want to be an eyeless ghost."

Marina and Kyle joined hands in front of a wide-eyed Sabine who was staring at them in a daze. Her eyes had become glassy, and Kyle was sure if the cape was not covering her hair, it would be floating wildly in the air.

"What do we do?" Kyle, who was trying not to freak out, asked Marina. He thought nothing more could freak him out after the time he was having. But this, this was no tame Harry Potter magic. This was more like Rose Mary's baby meets the Omen. If Sabine contorted backward with her head spinning around, he was out of there, ghostly form or not.

"Hold my hands and whatever you do, only look at me," Marina warned him.

What happened next was a bit of a letdown. Kyle was expecting the earth to rumble, a hell hole to open up, complete with an army of demons. Instead, Marina chanted a few words, and all the furniture in the room lifted up, and then thumped to the floor when Sabine dropped.

Kyle did not know whether to sigh in relief, be disappointed about the lack of demons, or mad he spent his precious time as a whole person holding some crazy lady's hand. He had no time to ponder over what had happened as he leaped forward, grabbing Sabine before she hit the hard floor.

///

SABINE'S HEAD ached as she opened her eyes. She had just had the strangest dream. She stretched out, wincing as her leg hit something hard, and making her sit straight up. It wasn't a dream! Sabine's eyes searched the room to find Marina talking to Kyle.

"Kyle?" Sabine called out, standing up too fast and nearly blacking out again. She plopped back down on the chair and put her head in her hands, trying to focus.

Kyle rushed over to Sabine, but he morphed back to ghostly form before he could reach out to her. "No way," Kyle muttered and then shuddered as he could feel himself dematerialize; it felt like inside-out goose bumps.

Sabine looked up at him. "How were you here in the flesh a moment ago?" she asked him curiously.

"Turns out your cape," Kyle pointed to the garment that was still on Sabine, "not only conceals magic. It is also filled with magic."

"I know that, but how did it make you whole again?" Sabine looked passed Kyle to Marina, who was going through numerous books that were all open on her desk.

"When Marina asked me for the cloak, I wished I could help you when you started to go all Carrie on us." Kyle smiled as she frowned at him, "And the cloak turned me into a real boy."

"Marina," Sabine stood up, going to Marina, "Can the cape help reunite Kyle with his body and save him?"

Marina stopped what she was doing and looked up at Sabine. "I'm afraid not, Sabine." Marina took off her glasses, "The cloak will only work once for a mortal."

"If I had known that, I would have made another wish," Kyle shook his head and huffed.

"Thanks a lot," Sabine made a face at him, "Nice to know that you are not a self-serving narcissist after all."

"You still have your body, your life, and your magic … soul … reaping … ability powers." He said, annoyed at her for judging him. "I'm the one who is dead and cursed."

"Through no fault of mine," Sabine shot back at him. "Yes, I may have been the one wielding the blade, but I most certainly was not the one who wanted you dead."

"No, of course not," Kyle sneered at her. "You were just doing your job like a good little soul-sucking reaper."

"Whatever." Sabine blew him off, her head ached badly, and she was no closer to finding her aunt.

"Okay, you two cut it out. You are going to attract attention." Marina came around the desk and took the cloak from Sabine to one again to cover Kyle. "We can't have anyone else here know we have a damned soul wondering about."

"Did I black out again?" Sabine asked Marina quietly.

"Yes, you did," Marina smiled at her reassuringly.

"What did Kyle mean I went all Carrie on you?" Sabine asked Marina. "It happened again, didn't it?" Sabine watched Marina closely.

"Yes, I'm afraid so," Marina reached out, touching Sabine's arm. "I managed to calm you down, but Sabine, dear, you need to learn how to control your fear, anxiety, and abilities," Marina warned her. "I may not always be around you, and you may not always have quick access to the Cape."

"I know." Sabine started to chew at her nails nervously. "I have been cautious to avoid situations that make me snap. I guess seeing my mother's book triggered a dark memory."

"Do you remember what it was this time?" Marina asked Sabine, staring at her as if she was trying to see into her head.

"I hope you are not trying to look at my memories again?" Sabine asked Marina, not liking the way she was staring at her. "You remember the last time you tried to look inside my mind and pull out some memories?"

"Yes, it took me months to get my magic back." Marina's brows drew together, "I have not found your mother's book of shadows amongst these books. I am still working on how to decipher that symbol and find something that will once again lock your powers away."

"Thank you, Marina," Sabine gave the woman a warm hug. "I know you will find a way. Any more information on the daggers?" Sabine shook her head, "I mean dagger."

"No." Marina said frustrated. "I will see what I can find out about lifting the enchantment. Once again, this is where your mother's grimoire would be useful." Marina smiled as Sabine. "I did check on Amalia's whereabouts, and she called in for a personal day today."

"That is just great, and on a day I need her," Sabine sighed. "I think I will go past her house and see if she is home to shed some light on all this."

"That is a good idea," Marina gave Sabine a farewell hug. "I will keep trying to find out what I can about the daggers."

FIVE

Breaking and Entering Astral Projection
Style

SABINE SAT IN HER SUV, LEANING ON THE STEERING wheel. Her head still ached a bit from her episode in the library. She hated getting what she called a memory flashback. They left her drained and frustrated because she never remembered what she had seen. She had tried to record one once, but the video was completely black with static. She had no time to ponder her problems right now; she had to find her aunt and Kyle's body. Time was running out; according to Marina, Kyle had until midnight that evening to have the curse lifted. If it could not be done, he was doomed to wander around like a lost soul. Sabine had a sneaky suspicion that she would be the one he would haunt.

The information that had her reeling the most was that the amber jeweled dagger belonged to Amalia. Sabine did not want to believe that Amalia could be responsible for kidnapping her aunt. There must be a logical explanation, but time was running out, and she needed answers.

"Are you okay?" Sabine jumped at Kyle's quiet question. For once, he had not moaned at her or shouted about his predicament. He had been so quiet she had forgotten he was even there.

"I am just worried about my aunt and cannot understand Amalia's involvement in all this." Sabine turned towards him.

"Marina told me that Amalia is your boss." Kyle told Sabine, "She was the one who talked you into going back into the family business after you lost your mother."

"Yes, that's right." Sabine smiled sadly, "Amalia was my mother's second in charge, so she was the most logical choice to take over the business." Sabine nervously chewed the skin around her very short nails.

"Why did you decide to join?" Kyle asked her curiously.

"Turns out the business is handed down from oldest daughter to oldest daughter." Sabine fidgeted in the middle compartment finding a roll of mints. "The overseers were not happy with me walking away. Aunt Lydia could not take over because my mom had me, an heir." Sabine took a deep brew and blew it out, looking straight ahead. "My mom wanted me to find my own path in life."

"That is what you were doing as an advertising executive?" Kyle asked, watching her.

"Yes," Sabine turned and smiled. "It was stressful, and Amalia assured me that this job would be less so." Sabine gave a small laugh. "You will be helping trapped souls find their way to the afterlife." Sabine rolled her eyes. "Well, at least that is how Amalia spun it to me."

"It sounds almost poetic when you put it like that," Kyle said, his forehead creasing as he asked. "Do you think Amalia will tell you why I was targeted?"

"She should," Sabine told him. "No soul can just be reaped because someone has a vendetta against another person. We are not assassins," she said defensively.

"Yet, you have never asked about why you were taking a person's soul." He looked at her with his ghostly eyebrows raised. "You get a file with a name, time, and location without knowing the why or anything about the person. It is also your job, so it sounds pretty much like an assassination to me."

"I don't take anyone's soul," Sabine told him, shaking as he attacked what her people did. "We are trusted to help a lost, forgotten, or trapped souls escape the prison of the flesh and moves on to where they are free."

"Free from what?" Kyle asked her. "Their lives?"

"We don't have time to sit here and argue about what I do," Sabine started the car. Kyle was getting all wound up again, and she did not need another upset right now. "For your information, it is not a job. It is a calling. It is what I was born as."

Sabine punched in an address on the GPS, and then backed out of the parking space heading in the direction the GPS instructed.

"We help souls move on and not get stuck here," Sabine explained as she headed towards Amalia's house. "There are many reasons why a soul can become trapped like you are now, a spirit, or inside their human vessel."

"So, you think I was trapped inside my human vessel?" Kyle asked Sabine, she felt his need for answers, anger, and fear inside him.

"It could have been the curse Elissa put on you," Sabine told him. "Maybe Amalia thought her dagger would be able to free your soul from the curse and help you move on." Sabine glanced at Kyle, who was staring out the window. "Living with a curse hanging over you can drive a person to do evil things. Or it can torture a person mentally, physically, or spiritually. It can topple your whole

RENEE JOINER

world and can even drive some to take their own life."
Sabine shuddered.

"I take it cursed souls that are not guided to a good
place end up in ... What? Hell?" Kyle frowned at her, "I
never much believed in hell until today."

"Listen, Kyle, I will do everything I can to make sure
this curse is lifted." Sabine swore to him, "You only get one
shot to move on to the afterlife, and I don't want to see you
stuck here like this." Sabine told him softly, giving him a
smile realizing at that moment that she had come to care
about Kyle. She also knew that she would do anything to
help him, even if it meant breaking protocol and taking on
the overseers and Amalia.

Sabine drove up outside a fancy apartment building
complete with a concierge in a fancy suit. "This is it."

Kyle whistled. "Wow, looks like being in the soul
reaping business pays well."

Sabine chose to ignore the insult and to not take it
personally. He had every reason to be angry and feel as he
did. "Most of our kind have been around for centuries, or
at least their families have. As a result, their wealth has
been amassed through time."

"I guess being magical beings has its advantages," Kyle
laughed at the look on Sabine's face. He reached out to
touch her hand, but his hand went right through hers. "We
will find your aunt and get answers, Sabine. If anyone will
get me through this, I believe it will be you," Kyle reas-
sured Sabine.

"Maybe you should wait here," Sabine told Kyle. "We
are not sure how involved Amalia is with this or why?"
Then why had been puzzling Sabine from the moment
Marina had told her it was Amalia's dagger.

"I don't like the thought of you going up there on
your own," Kyle told her, getting his stubborn look.

"What if you go all Carrie again and there is no one to help you."

"What do you mean going all Carrie?" She asked Kyle as it was the second time he had associated her with someone named Carrie.

"Have you not seen the movie Carrie based on the Stephen King novel?" Kyle asked her. "About this girl who had the power to move things with her mind?"

"No, I don't believe I have." Sabine told him, her brows drawn together in confusion, "I still do not understand why you would associate that movie with me?"

"Your episode where you zoned out and then things started flying around the room." Kyle looked curiously at her, "Wait, you don't know what you were doing."

"I …" Sabine pursed her lips and swallowed, "No, I get visions and have been told by those who know that I fall into a trace. None of them have ever told me that I make things fly around the room."

"That's strange because Marina poured a circle of salt around you, threw the cloak over you." Kyle watched her surprise as he continued, "Put that eye thingy around your neck and made me hold hands with her until you passed out."

"I wonder why Marina did not tell me this," Sabine said, now more confused than ever. "Maybe it was the first time it has happened?"

"I don't think so. Marina knew what to do right away like she had done it before." Kyle told her as they got out of the car. "One more thing." Kyle stopped her before she entered the building, "Marina seemed pretty intent on finding out about your mother grimoire."

"Oh, no, she needs it to try and bind my power to stop me from getting visions." Sabine explained, "With my mother gone, the binding spell she and my father put on me is fading." Sabine turned to Kyle, "Just wait in the car. I will not be long."

/ / /

THE CONCIERGE HAD LET Sabine into the building and typed in the code to get Sabine to Amalia's apartment. As the concierge had just come on shift, he was not sure if Amalia was home or not. There was a technician at the desk working on the faulty network system, so the concierge could not phone up to the apartment.

Sabine found Amalia's apartment with no problem as there were only two per floor. She rang the doorbell, but there was no answer. Sabine put her ear to the door to hear if any sounds were coming from inside, but there was nothing. She stood staring at the door, chewing on her lower lip while deciding whether to enter the flat or not.

Sabine looked around the passage and then placed her hand on the door and did something she never did—she used one of her many hidden powers. Closing her eyes, she breathed in; as she breathed out, she let herself meld with everything around her and astral projected into the apartment.

As she looked around, Sabine wished she had brought Kyle to keep an eye out on the hall, but as she hadn't. She had to be quick. She scanned the rooms, but they were all empty. There was no one home. Satisfied, Sabine drew her projection back. She hated this part as it made her feel physically ill. She felt all shaken and fizzy like putting Alka Seltzer into water.

Sabine stood, taking deep breaths to calm her tumbling belly and not throw up. Luckily, she had not eaten in hours, so there was nothing to throw up. She flicked her wrist, but the door would not open. That's strange, Sabine thought. She grabbed the doorknob to twist it, but a shock bolted up through her arm.

"Ouch!" Sabine shouted, immediately regretting it as the door to the apartment across the way opened.

"Are you alright?" A tall, exceptionally good-looking man answered the door. His eyes were the most startling whiskey brown. His hair was straight; short, thick, jet black, and well-groomed. Altogether, his face looked like it had been chiseled by the most accomplished artist, while his designer shirt clung to a well-defined chest.

Sabine swallowed, and her cheeks flamed as she realized she was staring, with her mouth open.

"I'm fine, thank you, just tripping over my own feet," she spluttered nervously, trying to find something to say.

"Have you hurt your hand?" he pointed to the hand she had cradled in the other one.

"I … uh …" Sabine cleared her throat. "No, no, it is fine. I hit it against the door when I fell." She showed him it was fine before shoving them behind her back. "Well, I best be getting along."

"Are you sure I can't have a look at that hand for you?" His voice was deep, rich, and hypnotic. Kike his eyes, they drew you in.

"Um …" Sabine licked her lips nervously and chewed her bottom lip. "No, I have to be going," she smiled at him, but she could not move for some reason. Her feet felt like they had become one with the floor.

"I'm Tatum," he said softly. A smile lifting his mouth and showing off deep dimples on either side of it.

"I'm …" Sabine swallowed again, her mind was like mush. "Sabine," she said, clearing her throat again. It was feeling dry, kind of like her vocabulary.

"It is nice to meet you, Sabine," Tatum looked down at her.

"Yes, well, I must be going," Sabine managed to get her feet extracted from the floor and walked towards the elevator, turning to give him a wave.

At the elevator, she realized she was stuck. She did not have a card key, and the communication system was not working.

Shoot. Sabine swore silently, looking around for the stairwell. The last thing she felt like was walking down seven or eight flights of stairs.

"Here, let me help you with that," the deep voice came from behind her, making her jump. "Sorry, I didn't mean to scare you."

He was as silent as a cat. Sabine had not heard or sensed his approach. As he leaned over her, his arm grazed hers. His alluring scent tantalized her senses, making her heart skip a beat and her skin heat.

"Thank you," Sabine squeaked and cleared her throat yet again.

What was her problem? She had been around men before. Not any like him, though. Her subconscious whispered to her.

"You are welcome," Tatum gave a slight nod. "I will see you down to the lobby. I have to get my mail and have a chat with Alex of the concierge."

Sabine could say nothing and stepped into the elevator, her legs felt like jelly.

"So, are you a friend of the woman who lives in the apartment across from me?" Tatum asked Sabine.

"Yes and no," Sabine told him. "She was a dear friend of my mother's and is now my boss after taking over my mother's position at the company." Sabine gave herself a mental shake. What the hell, Sabine? She never told strangers anything, but here she was jabbering to a stranger, but she felt almost compelled to tell him what he wanted to know.

Compelled? Sabine's eyes flew to meet those beautiful blue ones watching her intently. Tatum was a warlock. She instinctively took a step back. That is why she could not feel anything from him or sense him.

"Ah, I get it now," Tatum smiled knowingly at Sabine. Not saying anything about her, he suddenly moved away from where he stood.

The elevator door slid open. Tatum stepped out and held it for Sabine.

"Well, thank you for your help with the elevator," Sabine gave him a tight smile.

"You are welcome, Sabine. It was great meeting you," he nodded and gave her a small wave. As Alex let her out of the building, Sabine could feel him watching her.

As the door closed, she could have sworn he had said: "at last." She stopped and looked back. He was no longer staring at her but talking to the guy fixing the network. Sabine's hand still had tingles from the magic zap she had gotten, so she was probably imaging it.

"Are you going to stand there gawking at the door all day?" Kyle's impatient voice came from the vicinity of her car.

She turned around to see his spirit hovering by the passenger side door. "I thought I told you to stay in the car," Sabine hurried around to the driver's side. "Where is the cloak?"

Her question was answered when she noticed it lying across the passenger seat. To her surprise, Kyle morphed into the car and slid into the cloak.

"I see you learned a new trick while I was gone." Sabine laughed when he grinned at her.

"I wanted to see if you were okay but could not get out

of the cloak." Kyle told her, "As I figured it out, you came out of the building. I was going to see if I could fly up to the windows to see which one you were in."

"So, now you think you can fly?" she shook her head at him. "You have only just found out how to morph through things."

Sabine started the engine. Her skin prickled, so she turned her head to see Tatum standing at the doors watching her. In her haste to pull away, Sabine nearly hit a car that honked at her.

"Good grief, Sabine," Kyle shouted. "Who is going to drive us where we need to go if you end up a spirit too?"

"Sorry," Sabine breathed. She was a wreck, a wreck who had no clue where to find her aunt or Amalia. She was still no closer to figuring this all out as she was when her night from hell had begun.

"What did you find out?" Kyle asked her as Sabine started to drive.

"Nothing. Amalia was not home."

Sabine told him about having a look around and how she could not enter the apartment. She left out the bits about Tatum.

"So, Amalia has a magical anti-burglar device," Kyle made an impressed face. "Why couldn't you look when you astral projected?"

"I can't stay that way for too long," Sabine told him. Not really wanting to go into the details of why.

Her mind was reeling, and to top it all, she could not get Tatum out of her head.

"Do you think astral projecting could be classed as breaking and entering?" Kyle asked her. "You have some skills, lady," Kyle smiled at her. He was growing very fond of Sabine. "Who was the Greek God that followed you out of the elevator?" Kyle asked her.

"Not sure, but I think he is a warlock," Sabine told Kyle casually. "He is Amalia's neighbor."

Sabine pulled into a parking lot, switched off the engine, and jumped out, saying to Kyle, "I have to get a coffee and something to eat."

She also needed time to think and clear her head. This day just kept getting more and more twisted.

"Sure, I will just sit here in the car again, while you run off to a fast food truck to clog your arteries and get hyped up on caffeine." He gave her a tight smile.

"Yes, all that you just said," she told him sarcastically. Turning back, she quickly reminded him, "Stay here this time," and slammed the door.

SIX

Sabine, a Duck, and a Warlock

SABINE SAT IN THE PARK, EATING HER BAGEL AND DRINKING her coffee. She stared at the ducks swimming in the lake and kids playing ball with their dogs. It was a typically beautiful day. Well, for ordinary people, it was a typical day. For Sabine, it was a day of frustration, turmoil, and fear. She feared the worst for both Kyle and her aunt. Her mind was in turmoil because, apparently, she could throw things about with it. But mostly, she was angry and frustrated that every path they took was turning up as a dead end.

She was missing something here, well, not just something, full three-quarters of the puzzle. Sabine honestly had no idea where to turn to next or even start looking for the following clues. The dagger had turned up a dead end. All she knew about it was that it belonged to Amalia, who was not home, and after having made a few calls while sitting on the park bench, no one knew where she was or when she would be back. Kyle was running out of time, and Sabine had no clue what had happened to her aunt other than she was taken. If the red jeweled dagger also belonged to Amalia, had Amalia taken her? If so, why? It made absolutely no sense; maybe Amalia was also taken trying to help Lydia?

A brazen duck waddled out of the water and honked at Sabine, eyeing out the pretzel lying on her lap.

"No way, dude, this is mine." She finished off her bagel, picked up her pretzel, and took a huge bite of it. "You can't eat this. I took the one with salt." She showed the duck the bits of salt stuck to the weird shaped bread. It honked at her like it was upset. "I know right," Sabine shook her head. "I too wanted one without salt."

Sabine broke off a piece that did not have salt on. "Don't die, okay?" she told the duck that sucked the break up like a vacuum cleaner.

"Now you're trying to kill a duck?" Kyle's voice came somewhere from her side, and it gave her such a fright that she nearly fell off the bench. He reached out to grab her, but his hands went straight through her.

"Why aren't you in the car?" Sabine said, choking.

"I got tired of waiting and watching you sitting here, all sad."

"I am not sad, just upset that we keep running into dead ends." Sabine tore off another piece of pretzel and threw it for the duck.

"Well, murdering a duck is not going to be the answer," Kyle told her. "Let's start with what we do know."

"You were cursed by some woman you had a one night stand with," Sabine started to count on her fingers. "My aunt has been taken; my boss may or may not be involved in both your soul reaping and her disappearance." Sabine finished with, "We have no leads, no answers, or no more clues. We are dead in the water, and you only have until midnight tonight to get the curse broken."

"Yeah, that about sums up what we do know," Kyle agreed. "What we don't know is why I was cursed, who cursed me, if the green jewel carries any significance, and what is he doing here?"

"What?" Sabine looked up as Tatum ran towards her.

"Quick. Hide," Sabine looked around for somewhere to duck as Kyle faded off somewhere. "Lucky," she mumbled.

"Sabine?" Tatum ran over to her and tugged his ear buds from his ears. He was in his running shoes, loose jogging pants, and an open vest that showed off his powerful arms and lean trim muscled pectorals.

"Hi again," Sabine squeaked, raising her coffee cup to him. She did not know why she did that.

"Enjoying the warm morning, I see?" Tatum smiled down at her.

"Yes, just having a late breakfast and coffee," Sabine said, stupidly wishing he would run off now as she squirmed in his shadow.

"Well, I will leave you to it. Maybe we can grab a coffee together one day." He reached into his pants pocket and gave her his business card. "I was going to run to Amalia's office and ask the receptionist to give you this in hopes you would call me." Tatum smiled confidently.

"I hope I will see you again soon, Sabine," he said seductively, then took off, putting his ear buds back in his ear, all the while ignoring the admiring looks from everyone he ran by.

"Wow. Isn't he Mr. Smooth?" Kyle appeared next to her again.

"I see you are getting the hang of being invisible," Sabine eyed him, turning the card around in her hand, not bothering to look at it. "Your phone," Sabine looked at Kyle.

"What about my phone?" Kyle asked her, not realizing she had neatly steered the conversation away from Tatum.

"You said that you met Elissa using an app on your phone," Sabine said excitedly.

"Where are you going with this?" Kyle asked her; he could see the wheels turning in her head.

"Let's log in to the app on my phone using your profile, and you can show me what Elissa looks like." Excitement bubbled up in Sabine. If she could get the woman's face, maybe someone in her circles would know who she was.

"That is not such a bad idea," Kyle told her the app's name.

While they waited for the app to download, Sabine asked Kyle what he did for a living.

"I look after the woods that surround the area near my home," Kyle told her. "I have engineering, agriculture, and forestry degrees."

"Oh, wow," Sabine said, impressed. "So, do you just wander around taking care of the trees?"

"Kind of," he smiled, "But lately, I have been concerned about the number of poachers in the woods." He looked worried, "Now, I won't be able to check the traps."

"I'm sorry, Kyle," Sabine said softly. "When this is all over, I promise to help you with the traps."

"Thanks," Kyle said, watching as Sabine started to load the now fully downloaded app.

"There are three Elissa's on here," Sabine frowned, looking in Kyle's list of potential dates. "Wow, and each one of them a shapely blonde."

"Don't be jealous, Sabine. I am starting to rethink my choice of female hair color preference." He smiled as she automatically touched her auburn locks drawn back in a scruffy ponytail. Most of the silky mass was escaping.

"So, which one is she then?" Sabine asked, ignoring his chirp about her hair.

"She won't be in the potential dates." Kyle tried to grab the phone, making Sabine laugh as she scrolled through his comments.

"No wonder some woman cursed you," Sabine shook her head at him. "You should be more respectful of them. And so what if she had too many freckles." She tsked him, and then stopped. Her body going cold as she stared into the green eyes of a woman named Elissa.

"Is this her?" Sabine held up the phone for Kyle to see.

"Yes," he frowned at Sabine's peculiar reaction to the woman. "Do you know her?"

"She looks like the woman involved in my mother's disappearance," Sabine told him, images started to flash through her head. "Kyle …" Sabine wished she could grab his hand. "Kyle …" the panic began to rise in Sabine as she felt herself slipping away.

"Sabine!" Kyle shouted.

He had seen that look in the library just before Sabine had lost control. He looked around the park. There were families, ducks, and runners. Runners … Kyle looked around for the Romeo guy who was hitting on Sabine. She had said he was a warlock. Maybe he would know what to do.

"Sabine, listen to me," Kyle told her. "I need you to calm down. Do that centering breathing thing I have seen you do."

Sabine nodded. "Keep talking to me," she said, gripping the bench as if she was anchoring herself to reality. "Your voice is helping." Sabine breathed, trying to quiet her mind, but the pictures were rolling in all disjointed and making no sense. "Find Tatum."

"Hey, that was my idea," Kyle said. "But will he even see me?"

"Make him see you." Sabine felt like she was about to lose control when she heard a deep voice softly humming a melody her mom would sing to her. A tune that always seemed to make her calm, still her fears, and fall asleep.

"Just breathe, Sabine." A warm arm wrapped around her shoulders.

Keep calm little angel
Don't you fear
Nothing's going to get you here
Not as long as we are near
No matter where you are
We won't be far
Just close your eyes
Look into your heart
You will find us there
Breathe in deep
While you go to sleep
Safe in your dreams
No harm can come

The deep voice sang to her softly. She sighed and leaned her head against him, instantly falling into a calm sleep.

///

"LEAD ME TO HER CAR," Tatum told Kyle, gently scooping up Sabine's sleeping body.

"Sure," Kyle did not like him, but he was pretty sure that was more to do with the fact that he was feeling jealous of the guy rather than not trusting him.

"Did you get her phone?" Kyle asked Tatum when they got to the car.

"Yup," Tatum put it into the glove compartment of the car. "I'm going to stick around until she wakes up."

"Well, as you can see, I cannot stop you," Kyle slid into the vehicle but did not put the cloak on.

"So, what is going on here?" Tatum eyed Kyle suspiciously.

"I don't think I have the right to tell you that," Kyle eyed the man back.

This man just happened to pop into their lives right at this moment. It felt suspicious. Kyle was sure Sabine would agree with him. Right now, he and Sabine did not know who they could or could not trust.

"Fair enough. But when Sabine wakes up, you are both going to explain the daggers."

"What daggers?" Kyle asked Tatum innocently.

Tatum leaned over and removed the red jeweled one out of the glove compartment.

"These daggers," Tatum cut himself as he handled the blade. "Dammit," He applied pressure to his finger, "I will get some water."

That will teach him for sticking his nose in where it doesn't belong. Kyle smiled smugly as he watched Tatum walk towards a booth, nursing his finger.

Kyle wished he had hands to lock the guy out. Although, that was a pretty neat trick the way he hushed Sabine down from her episode. Kyle looked at Sabine propped against the driver's side window, sleeping.

She was stunning in an understated way. She had large hazel eyes, long auburn hair, and a small smattering of freckles across her nose.

He smiled, looking down at her chewed off fingernails. He could not remember how many times in the past hours he had wanted to take her fingers out of her mouth.

Sabine sighed and snuggled into the seat. She looked so

peaceful right now and was probably going to freak out when she saw that Tatum had come to help her.

A thought dawned on Kyle. How had Tatum known to come to help her? How did he know what to do?

Now, Kyle really wished he could lock the door. What if Tatum was the one behind all this? His eyes shot to Sabine. He needed to wake her up. An idea crossed his mind.

Kyle slipped into the cloak. He flapped his arms and found he could move the cloak.

He looked at Sabine, sleeping peacefully and muttered, "So sorry, Sabine."

He slapped her with the cloak, screaming, "Sabine, wake up" in her ear.

///

SABINE HELD up her hands defensively as something was attacking her. It sounded like a banshee screaming in her ear. She opened her eyes to see Kyle flaying the cloak around and hitting her in the face.

"What the heck is going on with you?" Sabine shouted at Kyle, touching her stinging face.

"I don't have time to explain," Kyle told her, "But I think we need to leave here now!" Kyle saw there was only one person in front of Tatum in the line.

"Okay," Sabine said, confused, looking for the keys, "Where are the keys?" she looked around the car. She found she was sitting on them. "Got them."

"Well, hurry then; it's time to go," Kyle saw that Tatum was now ordering.

"Is that Tatum?" Sabine pointed to the tall man buying water at the booth.

"Yes, now lock the doors," Kyle said, frantically trying to hit the lock with the cloak.

"What is going on?" Sabine's eyes bored into Kyle. "Why are you acting like there is an ax murderer after us. Did you anger another date?"

"Nope, but I think you just may have attracted the ax murderer." Kyle pointed to Tatum, sauntering towards them.

"What?" Sabine asked, her cheeks going red as she remembered nearly losing control in the park and calling Tatum.

"The long and short of it," Kyle watched the man getting closer to the car, "he appeared from nowhere. Sang you some sort of lullaby and you fell to sleep without raising the demons from hell this time."

The lullaby! Sabine remembered him singing it to her and nothing else. Her cheeks flamed once again.

"How did I get to the car from the park?" Sabine asked Kyle.

"Why I carried you, Sabine," Tatum told her as he hopped into the back of her car, offering her a bottle of water.

"How did you know that song?" Sabine asked him.

"That is a story for another day," Tatum told her. "Right now, I would like to know how you two are involved with Amalia."

"Why are you so interested in Amalia?" Sabine and Kyle asked Tatum at the same time.

"I asked first," Tatum laughed at the two of them staring at him like he had horns.

"I already told you how I know her," Sabine answered.

"Mm, I don't think you are telling me everything," Tatum's eyes started to go a deeper brown, drawing Sabine in. A slow smile spread across his beautiful mouth.

Sabine swallowed, feeling herself slipping into his mind. She could see the doorways as he beckoned to her, tempting her, drawing her in, as he stood just over the threshold.

"Sabine!" Kyle shouted. "Duck!"

"What?" Sabine was snapped back to reality with a thud on her windshield.

Sabine spun around to find the duck from the park. It was banging into the window like it was trying to break in.

"What the …" Sabine, Tatum, and Kyle sprung out of the car to go help the duck.

Tatum got to the duck first, but it went wild, flying at him and pecking him.

Kyle stood back, laughing at the ridiculous sight of the Don Juan fending off a duck.

"Kyle, help me," Sabine shouted to him, grabbing her jacket from the back seat.

"What should I do?" he held up his cloaked ghostly arms.

"It can sense you; go frighten it away," Sabine instructed, running around the car.

Sabine tried to throw her jacket over the hysterical duck, but missed and hit Tatum. That made Kyle laugh even more.

"Kyle!" Sabine admonished him, flapping her arms, trying to shoo the duck.

"I got it," Tatum reached out and expertly grabbed the duck. It was pecking furiously at his hands, so Tatum started to sing.

"Oh, come on!" Kyle looked on in disbelief as the duck calmed, put its head down, and fell asleep.

"What the heck was that about?" Sabine took the bird from Tatum to bring it back to the pond, placing it in one of the small bushes.

"I have no idea," Tatum said from behind Sabine as she gently stroked the feathery head of the duck, making sure it was okay.

"Poor little thing," Sabine stood up, dusting off her hands.

"I have to go. I cannot tell you my interest in Amalia, but what I can tell you is to be careful around her and her sisters." Tatum turned, put his ear buds back in, and started to jog towards his apartment building.

"Sisters?" Sabine called after Tatum, but he could not hear her.

✦ ✦ ✦

"THAT WAS WEIRD," Kyle said as Sabine got back in the car and started the engine. "I hope his finger rots. He tried to pick up the red dagger by the blade," Kyle laughed.

"We need to get back to the library. I need to know who that woman is," Sabine said, giving him a curious look, "How did he get the dagger?"

"Woman?" Kyle looked at her lost for a minute until it dawned on him. "Oh, you mean Elissa?" Kyle asked, trying to keep up. "Tatum found the dagger in the glove compartment."

"What was he doing in my glove …" Sabine shook her head. "Never mind. Right now, we need to find out who Amalia's sister is." A thought struck Sabine, and she turned the car onto the side of the road so suddenly that even Kyle nearly went flying.

"Hey, what is the problem?" Kyle looked around, "Are there more ducks?"

"Where is my phone?" Sabine searched through the compartments of the car.

"Here," Kyle pointed to the glove compartment. "Tatum put it in there when he put you in the car."

Sabine removed the seat belt and leaned over to get her phone. She went into the hookup app, scrolled to the picture of Elissa. She then went to her contacts and found Amalia's picture.

"Does she look familiar to you?" Sabine held up Amalia's picture from her contacts for Kyle.

"Yes, she looks a lot like Elissa," Kyle took a closer look. "Is it Elissa?"

"No," Sabine said, putting the phone down and pulling the car back onto the road. "It's my boss, Amalia."

"Oh," Kyle was thankful he was a ghost as Sabine zigzagged through the traffic. "I thought you were going to the library?" He asked as they turned onto the highway.

"No," Sabine moved into the far lane and put her foot down. "We are going back to my aunt's house."

"Okay …" Kyle sat back. "Why?"

"I need to know who took her," Sabine turned off onto the road to her aunt's house. "Then, I will figure out where she was taken to. Knowing who took her will lead us to your body as well."

'But we tried that, and you nearly asphyxiated," Kyle looked at her worriedly. "Remember?"

"I was not prepared last time," Sabine pulled into her aunt's drive. "This time, I will be."

Sabine reached over to the glove compartment and drew out some black silk gloves. Once she had put them on, she picked up both of the daggers. A blue electrical streak shot from the gloves when she touched the daggers.

"Holy moly," Kyle's eyes were wide as he automatically leaned away from the sparks.

"The daggers are filled with dark magic," Sabine held

them up. The blue electricity sparked up both handles. She looked like a magician from a Disney movie with their magic wands.

"You don't say," Kyle shook his head. This was the weirdest day.

SEVEN

The Return of the Darkness

"WHAT ARE WE LOOKING FOR HERE?" KYLE ASKED SABINE, giving her a wide berth while she held the flaming daggers, as he now thought of them.

"I need to do something I try not to do," She gave him a tight smile.

"Oh, no," he shook his head. "No, no, nooo." He was not equipped to handle preternatural Sabine.

"Don't worry," Sabine laughed, knowing he was thinking about the two episodes she had this morning. "This is nothing like that," she assured him.

Sabine opened the front door, took a deep breath, and stepped inside. This would not be easy for her; she had not done anything like this in years.

"That's okay," Kyle called from the door. "I will just wait out here, again."

Sabine turned, frowning at him before remembering the house was spelled.

"At least I know my aunt is still alive," Sabine sighed, relieved. "If she wasn't, you would have been able to cross the threshold."

"Oh, well, that is good news then," Kyle said sarcastically. "If the door is spelled, how could you walk in there with those daggers?" he asked.

Sabine looked back at him, then at the daggers. He had a point, no evil spirit, or otherwise, could cross that threshold, yet she had walked in with them. She walked back to Kyle, stepping outside next to him.

"Let's try something," Sabine grabbed hold of the cloak.

"Uh…" Kyle stared at her worriedly. "Is this where you suck my soul into that dagger?"

"Nope, but it's a tempting thought," Sabine said as she yanked the cloak and him through the door.

"Huh, look at that," Kyle said, looking around the house from the inside for a change.

"Sometimes you can be pretty useful," Sabine gave the cloak a few affectionate tugs. "Whoever carried that dagger in here knew my aunt. If they are dark artists, they were well cloaked."

"Like this cloak?" Kyle asked her. "I knew I did not like that, Marina."

"What are you talking about?" Sabine squinted at him. "What has Marina got to do with anything? She has done nothing but helped me with my problems and made my job easier."

"Or made hers a lot easier," Kyle said, folding his arms across his chest with his eyebrows rose.

"I think you are just overly suspicious of everyone in my world," Sabine accused.

"When you were rearranging the library earlier," Kyle began as he followed Sabine through the house, "she put that eye thingy on you and told it to do what it needed to do."

"I don't like the all-seeing eye," Sabine told Kyle as

she walked into the kitchen where she had found the dagger. "But she must have had her reasons for putting it on me. They can see what is plaguing your soul. She probably thought it would stop the nightmare I was trapped in."

"You were trapped in a nightmare?" Kyle asked her with concern before continuing. "She was very interested in that eye thing finding out about your mother's spell book."

"I think you heard wrong," Sabine shrugged his concern about Marina off. "I have daytime nightmares that I don't know how to get out of," Sabine shrugged. "Since Marina made me the cloak, I don't get lost in those dreams anymore."

"Are you sure that is all the cloak does?" Kyle watched Sabine pour a circle of salt on the ground.

Sabine stepped into the protective circle and placed the two daggers in front of her. She removed the black gloves and put them on either side of the two daggers.

"Do you need the cloak?" Kyle asked.

"Nope, but I am going to need you to keep quiet. No matter what you see or hear, you are not to say a word, step into, or break this salt circle," Sabine looked at Kyle. "Is that clear?"

"Crystal," he nodded.

SABINE CROSSED her legs and kept her core tight and back straight. She placed her hands on her knees and closed her eyes, concentrating on her breath. Her palms were facing up, and her hands open. She drew in the protection of her guide and animal spirit. Feeling their warmth and light spread across her palms, she closed her hands, crossed her wrists, and drew them up to her chest, softly chanting.

She straightened out her arms in front of her turning her palms down, and twisted them back up before opening her hands. She brought her hands together, gently cupping them. A golden ball of light appeared in the middle of the cupped hands, as the light grew, it started to spin. Sabine closed her cupped hands together, and the golden light squeezed out from between her fingers, growing as it spread up her arms. The light started to spin around her body before it vanished from sight.

Sabine's eyes had been closed through the entire process. She sat deadly still for a few seconds before the daggers in front of her started to vibrate. It looked like they were being shaken, and it was not long until everything in the kitchen began to shake. Sabine took a deep breath when she breathed out. Her head went back, her eyes and mouth opened, the light shot out from them.

The golden light flowed out of Sabine like a fountain. It flew upwards, before cascading down, forming a golden bubble of light over the circle of salt. Sabine slumped to the ground, as did the knives, landing in Sabine's hands.

///

KYLE INSTINCTIVELY DARTED FORWARD, shocked by what had just happened. He was sure he had seen this in some weird omen movie. Nothing good came from light spurting from a person.

"Don't!" a now familiar voice came from the kitchen door.

"You again," Kyle looked up at Tatum as he stepped into the kitchen.

"Why the hell did you let her do this?" Tatum walked carefully around the golden circle of light.

"Well, if you didn't notice, I don't have much say in anything," Kyle held up his ghostly hands. "What are you doing here? Are you stalking us?"

"Someone has to keep an eye on her, it seems," Tatum gave Kyle a dirty look. "And no, I am not stalking you or her. I came here to see Lydia."

"Lydia?" Kyle was now even more suspicious of the guy. "What do you want with Lydia?"

"We had business to discuss," Tatum looked around the kitchen. "Why isn't she here to guide Sabine?" Tatum hissed angrily.

"You don't know?" Kyle eyed the tall man.

"Don't know what?" Tatum asked impatiently as he went through Lydia's cupboards. "Where the hell does she keep the lavender?"

"What do you want to do with lavender? Have a bath?" Kyle said sarcastically.

"No, you fool," Tatum found the lavender. Pouring some into his palms, he crushed it before blowing it over the golden light. "It's for purification, peace, and protection."

"I thought that is what the light was doing?" Kyle asked curiously.

"No, that is what guides her and keeps evil out," Tatum explained, then turned to Kyle. "Who are you? And why are you and Sabine together?"

"Well, she killed me with a dagger. I did not die because I am cursed. My body was stolen the same time her aunt was taken." Kyle's eyes grew huge as he realized he could not stop talking. "What the hell?"

"Lavender is also used to relax, soothe, and help draw the truth out of people," Tatum told Kyle smugly.

"You bastard," Kyle cleared his thoughts. He was not going to let some warlock into them.

"Oh, relax," Tatum told him. "I know what I want to know now." Tatum waved his hand, breaking the spell.

※ ※ ※

SABINE STOOD behind her aunt as she opened her front door. But for some reason, she could not hear what her aunt or the visitor was saying. She could not see the visitor either. Her aunt was blocking her view. Sabine tried to step around her but couldn't. It was almost like her aunt was deliberately stopping her from seeing.

Frustrated, Sabine drew in her breath. She had to go deeper. Sabine knew it would be a risk opening another door, but she had to know what happened to her aunt and who took her. She closed her eyes and summoned her guide. The golden ball came to her, brighter, hotter, and thicker. This time she held it in her hands, lifted them above her head, then threw the ball into the air above her.

The golden ball of light spun wildly before bursting through the barrier, stopping her from seeing what her aunt had seen. She turned, this time she could see through her aunt's eyes. She gasped, "NO!"

The Darkness was at the door. This time, the red jewel from the dagger glowed from within it. But she could not hear what her aunt was saying, nor could she understand why her aunt was inviting The Darkness into her house. Sabine wanted to scream at her not to, but she had no voice here. This was only a vision. Being led by her aunt's actions, they walked into the kitchen, where her aunt made sweet tea.

How could The Darkness drink tea? Sabine was so confused. How could her aunt be friends with that thing that had killed her father? Sabine wanted to reach out and grab that red jewel. Somehow, she knew it to be significant, a source of power.

Could it be the thing's heart? Is that why she heard or felt a tortured soul when she had touched it? This did not make sense to her. Was her aunt part of what happened to her father? No! Sabine could not believe that … Unless…

It dawned on Sabine that maybe her aunt saw The Darkness as a person. But why did she not see the person? She needed to see the person.

Before Sabine could make sense of it, The Darkness slammed the table. Her aunt jumped up, but not before sliding something beneath the table. Sabine tried to bend to see what it was but she could not. She was linked to her aunt's vision.

The Darkness grabbed her aunt around the neck, holding the red jeweled dagger against her back. In the same position, they had found the mark on Kyle's body. She needed to hear what was being said, but all she could hear was roaring, the same noise she had heard in her nightmares.

Her aunt and the thing moved to the altar room, where her aunt had started to prepare Kyle's body for its burial. Sabine could not see much except that the body was shrouded by a dark swirling cloud, then it disappeared as did her aunt, leaving Sabine standing in the altar room.

She turned and ran to the front door but hit a barrier that bounced her back into the room. She banged on the barrier, screaming for her aunt, knowing she couldn't hear Sabine. Sabine could not see anything outside of the house. It was pitch black, and for some reason, her guide was not letting her follow her aunt out there.

The table! Sabine turned to go back to the kitchen, but

the golden light swarmed around her and dropped her back into reality.

/ / /

SABINE BREATHED in as she sat up and the golden bubble of light burst, then disappeared. Sabine immediately turned towards the kitchen table. She stood up to go see what was hidden there, but she could not pass the salt circle. She smacked into a barrier that glowed purple when she hit it.

Lavender? She turned around and came face to face with Tatum.

"You did this?" Her hazel eyes glowed with anger. "Let me out of here this minute," Sabine demanded.

"First, we are going to have a little chat," Tatum leaned casually against the counter, his arms crossed over his chest.

"I don't have time for little chats," Sabine said through gritted teeth. What was up with this guy? Who was this guy?

"I just want some truthful answers, Sabine," Tatum stared at her. "I came here to see your aunt only to be told she was taken."

Sabine turned and glared at Kyle, who shrugged saying, "He compelled me."

"Really?" Sabine shook her head at Tatum. "What did you want with my aunt?"

"Lydia and I were doing some …" Tatum searched for a word, "research together."

"Research on what?" Sabine's anger was starting to rise.

Their time was running short; she now knew her aunt was alive but in terrible danger. As was Kyle's soul. He needed to be near his body to break the curse. She did not need this jerk of a warlock getting in her way.

"That is between your aunt and me," Tatum told her. "If she did not tell you, it was because she was protecting you."

"Oh, just stop with all the cloak and dagger bull," Sabine's temper rose a notch; with it, things started to rattle all over the kitchen.

"Now look what you've done," Kyle shouted at Tatum. "Sabine, calm down."

"No, he needs to release me now," Sabine shouted. As she did, the daggers rose.

Sabine grabbed one of the daggers and sliced through the lavender barrier, the salt scattered, and the red jewel glowed. Red tendrils seeped out of the crystals and started to wrap around her hand. Her eyes changed from hazel to a light green-yellow before turning amber.

Sabine stepped out of the broken circle of salt, dagger clutched in her hand as she advanced on Tatum.

"You had better start giving me answers," her voice was soft but held a severe threat. The closer she got to Tatum, the thicker the red tendrils now curling up her forearm got.

"Sabine …" Kyle stepped in front of Tatum. "Put the dagger down." Kyle stood his ground, not liking the look in her cat's eyes. "Please."

"I can handle this," Tatum stepped around Kyle. He opened his hand in which he had a yellow powder that he blew at Sabine.

Sabine shook her head. She looked disorientated for a while, then confused. She looked down at her hand. The red was subsiding. She dropped the dagger onto the floor, swaying and grabbed the kitchen table for support. Making her way to a particular kitchen chair, Sabine sat down. She needed a distraction to feel beneath the table.

"Where did you get these?" Tatum pointed to the daggers, careful not to get too close to them.

"It's a long story," Kyle told him, going over to Sabine, "Are you okay?"

"I'm fine," Sabine gave Kyle a thankful smile. "But, I could not see who took my aunt. All I know is that she is in danger. Whoever has her wants you in exchange for her."

"How do you know that?" Kyle asked her.

"The dagger," Sabine swallowed; trying not to think of the pain she had felt from whatever was trapped in that dagger.

"So, they are leaving a trail of daggers like crumbs leading us to a house of candy so we can be locked in an oven and eaten by the big bad witch?" Kyle breathed angrily.

"Why are you getting so angry again?" Sabine snapped back, finding her perfect distraction. "I am the one doing all the work. I have been doing everything in my power to piece this mess together." She ended up raising her voice.

"Well, that is the hazard of your shitty job," Kyle told her nastily. "You reap what you sow, honey."

"This is not my fault, you bastard," Sabine shouted back at him. "You are the one that dissed the wrong woman and got your sorry soul cursed."

"Nice," Kyle sneered at her. "You hardly know anything about me. So, you have no business judging me."

"Enough!" Tatum slapped down hard on the kitchen table.

Well, that went a lot better than she expected. A piece of paper dropped into Sabine's hands from the bang.

"I think it is about time the two of you told me what the hell is going on here." Tatum gave them a look that would make the devil himself come to heel. "Seeing these daggers, I am pretty sure you both have somehow gotten yourselves involved with something dark."

"We don't have time to sit here and give you a play by play," Sabine dismissed Tatum. She needed him to leave so she could find out what she had in her hand. "If you want to know, you will have to come with us."

"With you where, exactly?" Tatum asked her.

"I need to go back to the library to find out what Marina knows about a woman named Elissa," Sabine scooched off the chair hidden by the table.

Sabine snatched up her gloves, putting them on and hiding the note, before picking up the daggers.

"Did you say, Elissa?" Tatum stopped, his face turning white.

"Yes ..." Sabine stopped, looking at Tatum with raised eyebrows. She could feel emotions toiling through him. Her brows furrowed. Sabine tilted her head to decipher it, but he blocked her. "You know her?"

Sabine pulled her phone out of her pocket, scrolled through it, found the picture, holding it for him.

"Is this her?" Sabine asked.

"I ..." Tatum stuttered. It was the first time she had seen him flustered.

"Never mind. Even the waiter at the restaurant was flustered by her." Sabine snapped off her phone, "And I am pretty sure his sexual orientation did not lean towards women, but I think for her, he would convert."

Who the heck was this woman? Clearly, Amalia was not Elissa? Was Amalia Elissa's sister? Why did Tatum warn her about the sisters? What were these daggers? So many questions to be answered and Sabine had little time to find them.

Sabine looked at the two daggers she held in her hands.

She could feel pain, guilt, torment, and so many tortured feelings emanating from them. Whatever magic had forged them was of the darkest kind, and as old as time, she was sure of it.

"Wait," Tatum called Sabine as she turned to leave the house with Kyle. "How do you know about Elissa?"

"She was the one who cursed him," Sabine pointed to Kyle. "Let's go, lover boy," Sabine grabbed the cloak, pulling Kyle through the magical barrier. "Lock up when you go," Sabine called to Tatum over her shoulder.

"Wait," Tatum called to Sabine again. "I'm coming with you."

Sabine stopped, sighing, great now she had two of Elissa's conquest following her around. She was going to kill Amalia herself for getting her involved in this.

"Shotgun," Kyle called, phasing into the front seat.

"You do know I can just sit on top of you?" Tatum drawled, climbing into the back of the car.

The two men were so busy arguing none of them noticed Sabine carefully slipping off the black gloves and burying them with the note deep in the glove compartment.

"Buckle up, buddy," Kyle laughed, watching Tatum grabbing for the seat belt as Sabine screeched out of the driveway.

EIGHT

Breaking Protocol

BOTH OF YOU HAD BETTER START TELLING ME EVERYTHING you know about this Elissa woman," Sabine hissed. She was now fed up with running around in circles. Her aunt was in immense danger, Kyle was about to become a lost soul, and she knew nothing about the warlock in her car.

"We had a few dates," Kyle admitted. "It was after our third date when that mark appeared. She only ever wanted to meet at the Old Church restaurant."

"So, you went there more than once?" Sabine looked at Kyle. "Why didn't the waiter tell me that?"

"He was only there on the third night. I don't remember seeing him the other times," Kyle told her.

"Was there something different about the third date?" Sabine asked. She knew she was pushing.

"Yes, we had sex," Kyle told her bluntly. "In the grave-yard behind the restaurant."

"Oh …" Sabine's cheeks flamed as a green emotion, gripped her heart.

"I'm sorry I did not tell you," Kyle said softly. He hated telling her that. It was at that moment he realized he was falling for Sabine. How ironic was that? He had to die to find the one person worth living for.

"I understand," Sabine told him. "But you should have told me sooner. It would have saved us a lot of time." Sabine turned the car around and headed for the graveyard.

"I could not bring myself to tell your aunt that," Kyle smiled sadly. "I felt embarrassed."

"I hope you remember which grave it was as that could be significant to this mystery," Sabine said.

"I think so. It was an ancient grave," Kyle shuddered, thinking about it now. Amazing how alcohol made everything seem exciting at the time. "With a huge looming statue of a weird looking angel and the soil on the grave was new."

"The graveyard?" Tatum could not keep quiet any longer. "You idiot."

"Look, buddy, I don't remember including you in this cover …" The heat started to burn through Kyle's wrists, the pain searing his soul. "Sabine, I feel like I am on fire…"

Sabine looked over at him, shock vibrating through her.

"Kyle?" She looked around for the bottle of water Tatum had given her earlier.

Deep down, she knew those flames could only mean a few things, but her heart refused to acknowledge them. Trying hard to keep the car on the road, her hands shaking, Sabine managed to twist off the water bottle cap. She poured the water over Kyle's wrists to douse the flames, but the water passed through, wetting the cloak and the seat. The flames grew brighter, forming a fiery infinity loop around Kyle's writs as he screamed in agony.

"Sabine," Kyle shouted. "Help me, please," he called

desperately before starting to sink through the car seat like he was being dragged underwater.

Sabine slammed on the brakes, grabbing for Kyle, but all she got was the cloak left behind on the wet seat.

"Do something," Sabine shouted at Tatum with urgency in her voice.

"There is nothing I can do, Sabine. You know how magic works," Tatum watched. Feeling sorry for Kyle as he knew how painful the Flame of Infinity was.

"Damn you," Sabine hissed at Tatum, jumping out of the car shouting for Kyle. She knew it was irrational, but she knelt to look under the car, hoping he would be there. "Kyle," Sabine cried, feeling beneath the vehicle for him.

"Sabine," Tatum reached out, pulling her up from the road. "He's gone."

"No," Sabine shook her head. Fighting against Tatum, she twisted free. Tears now streaming down her face, she ran around the car, ducking down, checking for Kyle as she called out for him.

"Sabine," Tatum shouted. "We need to go. You are in the middle of the road."

Sabine stopped, standing up, her eyes started going from hazel to a yellowish-green before turning amber. The escaped tendrils that fell freely around her face raised as the power began blazing through her. The ground shook, cars skidded to a stop, dust and rubble on the road swirled, picking up momentum as they turned into a funnel of debris.

Sabine's eyes locked onto Tatum, who stood holding up his hand defensively, eyeing her and the humans all around them, including children and the elderly.

"Sabine, calm down," Tatum said softly. "You are breaking protocol, and you know what that means." Tatum looked at the attention she was drawing. He flicked his wrist, cloaking Sabine and himself while distorting the onlookers' memories of what they had witnessed. While Sabine's power fed off the rage, fear, and uncertainty inside her, the road behind them burst open, creating a giant sinkhole from which a torrent of water exploded.

"You," Sabine advanced on him. The funnel of debris growing in strength behind her. "This is your fault," she hissed. Her chest rising and falling as all her stress and anxiety were being released through her anger.

"No," Tatum told her, patiently fending off objects flying at him from the funnel. "No, I did not start this, Sabine. Deep down, you know that." Tatum kept his voice soft and soothing. "You are hurt, angry, and frustrated. I can help you if you let me, Sabine. You just have to calm down."

Tatum's power was being divided by fending off dangerous items hurtling at him, making sure no human was harmed, and keeping up the smokescreen. He was powerful, but her power was something else altogether. Without his full strength, he did not know how much longer he would be able to hold her at bay.

"Tell me about Elissa," Sabine stared at him. Her eyes were now the color of deep gold; the SUV shook as she moved past it towards Tatum. "Tell me what I want to know now."

"Sabine," Tatum kept his voice low, patient, and calm disguising the fear pumping through his veins. "Please, you have to calm down."

"Calm?" Sabine stood looking at Tatum. "Calm?" she laughed angrily. "Do you know how many times I hear that word a day?"

She lifted her hand out, flipped her wrist, balling her fingers into a fist. An invisible noose locked around Tatum's neck, his hands immediately went to his throat.

"Sabine," he said hoarsely. "Don't do this. There are going to be consequences."

"Consequences?" Sabine laughed again. "I have lived with the consequences of this demon inside of me my entire life." She yelled, squeezing her fist and yanking it down.

Tatum dropped to his knees, gripping his throat with his one hand and steadying himself against the SUV with his other. His power was waning fast. He did not know how much longer he would be able to maintain his magic cover.

"Please, Sabine, I will tell you what you want to know but not here," Tatum looked at her, not liking the look on her face, not to mention the alarm he had felt when he saw her color eyes. Now he realized what he was up against and knew even at full strength that he would be no match for her on his own if she truly let go.

"Who is Elissa?" Sabine scooted down on her haunches, lifting his head with her free hand. "Where will I find her?"

"I told you," Tatum swallowed and gasped for breath. "I will tell you what you want to know when you have calmed down."

"You know I can just find out what I want, right?" Sabine gave him an evil smile. "All I have to do is open the door to your third eye and climb into your head."

"That won't help Kyle or your aunt," Tatum's throat ached as he gasped for breath. The magic noose getting a notch tighter.

"Kyle is one of the reasons I am in this predicament," she shouted. "I never wanted to come back to this life. I walked away but was roped right back into it because of your kind." Anger blazed through her. "It was all fine, not great, but fine up until I met Kyle," she said his name with both rage and pain.

Sabine stood up, swayed, grabbing her head as pain echoed through her brain. Sabine staggered, leaning against her car, dots flashed before her eyes, and a soft, soothing voice echoed through her head.

Breathe, Sabine. Breathe. The voice soothed her.

Her anger simmered down, the swirling funnel dropped to the ground, and the world around her came into focus.

Oh, no! What have I done? Sabine could see through the magic veil Tatum had cloaked them with.

There was a big hole in the road where water shot out of the ground. People ducked for cover into the shops that lined the streets, while drivers abandoned their cars. She had caused a complete mess of one of the main streets in the city.

"Sabine," Tatum called to her. "I can't keep the cloak up for much longer."

Sabine turned to find Tatum kneeling on the road, gasping for breath with his hand on his throat. She looked down at her hands; one was balled in a fist. She opened it like she was throwing down something terrifying. The invisible stranglehold on Tatum was broken, and he fell forward, taking deep, ragged breaths.

"I'm sorry," Sabine dropped down next to Tatum, helping him stand up.

"We need to go," Tatum told her, still holding his neck.

Sabine nodded, running around to the driver's side of the car. As they drove off, the emergency vehicles arrived to clean up the chaos they had caused in the street.

"You can't go blowing up like that in full public view." Tatum tugged on the seat belt and settled into the passenger seat. He flicked his wrist to dry it and his now wet jeans off.

"When this mess is sorted out," Sabine said with conviction, "I'm done with this life." Sabine turned onto the road that led to the Old Church restaurant. "I never wanted to come back to it in the first place."

"Sabine, you know it is not that simple to walk away from what you are," Tatum said softly.

"Trust me, I do know," Sabine looked at him with determination in her eyes. "I did it once, but this time, I will do it right."

"What is that supposed to mean?" Tatum looked at her worriedly. Undoubtedly, she knew with that kind of power, the Elemental Magic world would never let her walk away.

"Do not concern yourself with my problems," Sabine told him, "I am not sure who you are or how you are involved in all this. But right now, you are the only lead I have, so I think you should start talking."

"I will answer your questions if you answer mine." Tatum bargained.

Sabine pulled up into the graveyard's parking lot, which was at the back of the Old Church restaurant. As there were still some families that frequented relatives' graves, the restaurant owner had created a separate entrance to the cemetery.

"Fine, but I get to ask first," Sabine reached back for the cloak Kyle had slid out of when he was ripped from the car.

"No," Tatum stopped her from reaching for the cloak. "You don't need the cloak."

"The cloak is what keeps me from becoming a crazed ball of power," Sabine withdrew her wrist from Tatum's hand. Something felt different or off with him.

Sabine yanked the cloak from the seat only to drop it

again when Kyle's fear vibrated off it and straight through her.

"Sabine, are you okay?" Tatum grabbed her upper arms as her face paled.

"I could feel Kyle's pain and fear," Sabine breathed. Tears welling up in her eyes.

"None of this is your fault, Sabine," Tatum assured her, feeling the guilt and anguish rising within her. He could also feel that it went a lot deeper than just Kyle and Lydia.

Sabine sniffed, wiping the tears from her eyes. She was not cut out for this life; all she wanted was to feel like a normal person with a normal life. Her previous job may have been stressful and even soul-shattering, but it was normal, filled with normal souls.

"I was the one who put Kyle in this position and inadvertently got my aunt involved," Sabine removed the keys from the ignition before reaching over Tatum for the daggers.

"So, I am more than a bit at fault," Sabine was careful not to touch the jewels that adorned the top of the handle on each knife. "Kyle was right. I never bothered to find out why my assigned souls were being reaped. I was content to believe what we were told." She placed the daggers in her belt and pulled her shirt over them.

"You would not be given the reason even if you asked," Tatum climbed out of the car and followed her to the cemetery gates. "You know the rules of the high reapers."

"That's right. We are only allowed to know that we are helping trapped souls find peace and safe passage to the afterlife, freeing them from the confines and pollution of the flesh," Sabine mockingly recited the training instructions reapers were given. "Maybe if I had done a bit more research on the targets, I could have stopped whatever is happening here."

"Do you know what is happening here?" Tatum asked her as they entered the graveyard.

"I know that Kyle was cursed by a woman that has some ancient power." Sabine stood, looking around the area. Her hand rose to her mouth, and she chewed what little nails she had left. "I have a feeling he was cursed here in this graveyard for a reason."

"Okay, well, I guess that is a start," Tatum smiled, watching her chew off more of her nails. "You need to stop biting your nails."

"Oh," Sabine removed her hand from her mouth, "Bad habit." She gave Tatum a tight smile, her cheeks going bright red.

"So, what are we looking for?" Tatum asked her as they started moving between the graves.

"I think I will know it when I see it," Sabine ran her hands over some of the gravestones as she walked through the neat paths. "Some of these graves are old."

"Yes, I can feel the sorrow and pain of all those left behind to mourn them," Tatum shivered, again watching Sabine as she gently touched each stone, bending down to the ones on the ground.

"Really?" Sabine looked at Tatum, surprised. "An empathic warlock?"

"There is a lot about me that you do not know, Sabine," Tatum laughed at her insinuation about magic practitioners being insensitive to others' feelings.

"Well, then tell me a bit more about yourself, Tatum," Sabine turned, walking backward to look at him.

"Are you sure that's a good idea?" Tatum's brows drew together worriedly as he watched Sabine.

"What?" Sabine smiled at him teasingly. "Me walking backward or you telling me more about yourself?"

"Both, I guess," he made a face raising his hand protectively as Sabine only just avoided indentations or obstacles on the grassy path.

"You know for someone who is always demanding answers, you are not very good at giving them," Sabine spun around, carrying on the walk with her back to him.

"I am not used to being on the other side of an interrogation," Tatum shrugged, relief flooding him because she was now watching where she was going.

"Is that what you were doing to me and Kyle?" Sabine stopped in front of a grave.

"If I am honest, at first, yes," Tatum looked at her curiously, wondering why she had stopped.

Sabine ran her hand over the gravestone, she closed her eyes. She could hear the whisperings of the lost. Sabine never feared them. She had always wanted to try and help them. Only, she was never allowed to as protocols dictated she could not.

For centuries, light soul reapers and dark soul reapers had grudgingly worked around each other. The councils of both sects like to call it a working together scenario. But the two sects knew not to cross the lines or protocols that were in place to keep the peace. It was more of a "you don't interfere with my job, and I won't interfere with yours" situation.

Some souls could not be saved, but those souls did not deserve to become hunted and terrorized by dark reapers. Granted, some people did terrible, heinous things as humans, but what the dark reapers did to their souls was beyond barbaric. Those dark souls were supposed to be put through a sort of rehabilitation in a prison world. But Sabine had never once known of a dark soul to ever be released from a prison world.

The lost souls were those the reapers could not get to; they were a grey area between the light and dark. Like the souls that bore a curse, had taken their own life, or those that had been murdered. The lost souls also, unfortunately, included those that had an accident or a sudden fatal disease and were taken too soon. Light reapers were not allowed to help them, and dark reapers were not allowed to take them. But they could torment them, either drive them to commit an offense or go insane. Once a soul had flipped, they were fodder for the dark reapers.

Lost souls spent their time in torment linked to where they were buried or where they died if they were cremated. The only way they could leave the area is if someone acknowledged them and allowed them to follow them, like Kyle and her. Most dark reapers loved to play with these lost souls like a cat playing with mice. What Sabine had done with Kyle broke all their protocols and rules. So it had been a rule-breaking day for her.

"Sabine?" Tatum's deep voice drew Sabine out of her thoughts. "Why are we stopped here?"

"Give me a minute," Sabine said softly, keeping her eyes closed and concentrating on listening.

The stone Sabine held emanated with such sorrow that tears rolled down her cheeks. Images of all those who had attended the grave walked through her mind. She could feel all the grief poured into the soil with the tears that had dropped onto it.

The soul trapped in this grave had reached out to her as she had wandered through the graveyard touching the stones, putting a question out to the lost ones that lingered here. The soul in this grave wanted Sabine to see the pain and suffering caused by...

NINE

The Charm Bracelet

SABINE'S EYES FLEW OPEN. SHE YANKED HER HAND OFF THE gravestone, slowly turning around. Tatum was standing staring at her, his eyes boring into her.

"Are you okay, Sabine?" Tatum asked her, taking a step towards her.

Sabine swallowed and automatically took a step back, ramming into the headstone.

"Uh, I…" Sabine was drawn into a vision before she could say anymore.

In Sabine's mind's eye, she could see a man and woman in a passionate embrace. They were kissing fervently, not able to keep their hands off each other, pulling at each other's clothing. They fell to the ground right in front of a grave, and as they did, Sabine saw Kyle's face.

"Kyle," Sabine whispered. Opening her eyes, she stepped past a wide-eyed Tatum to look up at the grave opposite them.

A seven-foot statue towered over a grave, and it looked

like it had been newly or recently dug up. But the statue was no angel. It was a statue of Nocheli. The creature that both light and dark reapers had once feared. The reason that the two sects had eventually allied. Nocheli was like the vampire of the soul world. She fed on the lost souls. They were a snack to keep her sated while she hunted fresh prey that still breathed. It was the souls of the living that gave her immortality and ensured she never aged.

Sabine shuddered as she remembered the stories told about Nocheli. She would portray herself as an angel; lull her prey into a false sense of security. At the same time, at night, Nocheli would feed off their souls until all the life force was drained. She became the thing of folklore, called a soul eater of which many myths arose.

"I think it was a follower of Nocheli that cursed Kyle," Sabine said, feeling herself being drawn towards the statue as it called out to her.

"No, Sabine," Tatum stepped in front, stopping her from stepping on the grave and touching the statue.

"It wants to tell me something," Sabine stood staring past Tatum almost as if in a trance.

"No, Sabine," Tatum grabbed her by the upper arms and shook her. "That statue never just wants to tell someone something."

"What?" Sabine looked confused for a minute. Realizing Tatum held onto her, she yanked back, ripping herself out of his hands. "Who is Mathews?"

Tatum paled. He stepped back like Sabine had slapped him, and then looked past her to the gravestone she had touched.

"How do you know that name?" he asked her, looking at her with a furrowed brow.

"Answer the question," Sabine took another step back away from Tatum and the dark evil's looming statue.

"One of Elissa's victims," Tatum said quietly, looking past Sabine, not able to look her in the eye, knowing she would read him.

"Elissa's victims?" Fear flashed in Sabine's eyes as she put more distance between herself and Tatum. "Who is Elissa to you, Tatum?" Sabine asked him.

"Sabine, let me explain," Tatum tried to take a step towards her but stopped as he noticed her hands balling into fists next to her sides.

"Answer the question, Tatum," Sabine's chest rose and fell as she backed away from him, looking towards the graveyard's exit. She formulated a plan to slow him down, knowing there was no way she could outrun him.

"Sabine, don't run," Tatum told her warningly. "Let's have that talk we were starting to have."

"I don't think so." Sabine was not sure if she would be able to gain her power so soon after the last bout. Truth be told, she was unsure how to control it or even switch it on and off. That is why she had the cloak Marina had made for her. To stop her from losing control and absorbing the energy around her.

"Sabine, I am warning you. You don't want to do this." Tatum watched her like a hunter cornering their prey.

"You were in the car when Kyle got taken." It all started to click into place for Sabine as the whispers swirled around her. "You spelled Amalia's door handle, but it was not meant for her but me." Sabine kept backing up, and Tatum kept walking forward. "You knew I was going there."

"Sabine," Tatum warned her. "I am asking you nicely to please stop so we can talk this out."

"It was you," Sabine's eyes grew big as Tatum's vision wielding a dagger played in her mind. "You cursed Kyle."

Anger rolled inside of her, her eyes flashed gold. The

ground started to vibrate, disturbing the sleeping souls. The whispers turned into moans as the lost emerged from their resting place. Sabine hunched down; touching the ground, she closed her eyes and chanted. She could feel the dead's cold swish by her, and her fingers started to ache as the ground became icy.

Run, Sabine, run. The whispers told her.

She heard Tatum shout but did not look back. She turned and bolted through the cemetery gates. She heard them slam shut as she was through them. Sabine fumbled for her keys in her jeans' back pocket, making it to her car as she fished them out. She jumped into the SUV, automatically locking the doors. Her hands shook so much that she was thankful for the automatic starter buttons she had first cursed. Without daring to look back, Sabine screeched out of the parking lot and gunned it. Her sole intent was to put as much distance between her and Tatum as she could, as fast as she could.

//*/*

SABINE'S MIND REELED. This was one of the most awful days of her life. A simple assignment had turned into a twisted web of lies, deceit, and ancient curses. Sabine needed to get back to the library before it closed for the day. Sabine glanced at the clock on her dashboard. It was now a quarter past two; she had two hours to get there. First, she needed to make a quick stop at a spot she had not been in a while.

Sabine turned into a street lined with old cherry trees. She drove up to large wrought-iron gates. Leaning out her car window, she typed in a keypad code, and the gates slid open. Sabine took a deep breath; as she drove up the long drive, tears stung her eyes, and her heart felt heavy as it always did when coming home. She missed her parents so much; she could not believe they were now both gone.

Sabine pulled up outside her childhood home. It was the only place she could think of to go and sort out her mind. She also needed a quick shower, change of clothes, and something to eat. Mary, the housekeeper, always kept the house stocked in case Sabine came for a visit. Mary! A thought struck Sabine. Mary had been her mom's nanny. She may be able to help Sabine sort through some of this mess. What Sabine was able to find out was that Kyle and her aunt were okay for now. However, come nightfall, they would not be.

Sabine felt drained. She needed a cup of chamomile tea and a donut with a thick ring of caramel surrounding it. She also needed to go back in time and not take this job. She was much better off at the advertising agency in hindsight. At least, there she did not have to deal with dark magic, curses, tortured souls, and missing aunts.

How the heck had her life gone so awry? Her mother had taken pains to make sure Sabine was free of this life. Sabine's hand automatically went to her throat, where her mother's necklace had given her used to hang. She had not taken the necklace off since she was a young girl until it broke a month ago.

As Sabine was about to get out of the SUV, one of the daggers jabbed her back. She had been in such a rush to get away from that crazed warlock that she had forgotten to put them in the glove compartment. She took them out of her belt and shoved them in.

The note. Sabine had nearly forgotten about the note inside her glove. She grabbed the glove and shook it, but the note was gone. She checked the other one, but there was nothing. Had Tatum taken it? She could not remember him having enough time to. Anger started to boil inside her again. Just when she thought she had a lead, poof, it vanished. She threw the gloves back into the compartment, and something thudded. Curious, she looked into the cubby; a blue velvet box caught her attention.

That was not in there before. Sabine reached in and pulled it out, opening it with caution.

It was her mother's charm bracelet that had gone missing years ago. She could remember asking her mom where it had gone, and all her mom had said was that things lost are found when they needed to be.

Sabine was not convinced that it had magically appeared in her car. Did Tatum put it in there? But how? She had known it was not in there at the cemetery when she got the daggers out. Tatum had not had time to put it in her car. Her car was also spelled; only those closest to her could magically touch her in the car. Both Kyle and Tatum would not have been able to get this into her car without her seeing it.

Sabine was deep in thought, staring at the bracelet as she climbed the stairs to the front door. She nearly died of fright when Mary swung the door open, immediately engulfing her in a hug.

"Sabine," Mary's pudgy cheeks dimpled in a big smile as she led Sabine into the house.

"Hi Mary," Sabine greeted the woman, shutting the box, "I need a quick shower, some tea, and some of your Beignets if you have any."

"Well, now love, you know I always have those awaiting you." Mary guided Sabine to the stairs, "You go freshen up while I get you something to eat. You are all skin and bones, child." Mary clucked before going off towards the kitchen.

/ / /

SABINE SAT at the kitchen table, drinking some sweet tea and wolfing down her second helping of Beignets. While she had showered, she had gone over the day's events trying to put bits and pieces together. The most information she had gathered was from the lost souls in the old cemetery.

She still did not know why Kyle was cursed, what it had to do with that grave with the statue of Nocheli looking over it, and what Tatum's part in all this was. That was the grave where Kyle had been with that Elissa woman or demon. Every time she thought of Kyle with her, Sabine thought spitefully she got a horrible twinge of jealousy followed by a bout of anger at Kyle's stupidity.

"Sabine," Mary called, snapping her fingers, "Honey, are you still here with me?"

"Oh, sorry, Mary, it has been the most awful day," Sabine sighed, leaning her head against her hand, her long, dark, newly washed hair sweeping forward like a curtain.

"Do you want to talk about it?" Mary rubbed Sabine's back comfortingly as she did whenever Sabine was troubled.

"I don't want to get another loved one involved in all this, Mary." Sabine hugged the woman, "I would hate for anything to happen to you too."

"Happen to me?" Mary looked at Sabine worriedly, "Well now, young lady. I think you need to start talking." Mary pulled up a chair plopping down on it and folding her arms. Letting Sabine know she would not be leaving the table until she knew everything. "And where is your necklace, love?" Mary asked.

"Oh, it got broken." Sabine reached for another donut but got an apple placed in her hand by Mary instead, "It got caught on Marina's jumper and snapped."

"Where is it now?" Mary asked, looking at Sabine strangely.

"It is with Aunt Lydia." Sabine smiled at Mary, understanding why she would be concerned, "Don't worry, Mary, I have everything under control." Sabine took a bite of the apple, "Besides, Marina made me a cloak to help on missions, and it calms me down if I feel I am starting to lose control."

"A cloak?" Mary raised her eyebrows, "May I see this cloak."

"Don't worry so much, Mary. Marina spelled it for me, so we know it is perfectly safe." Sabine shrugged off Mary's suspicions. "Why is everyone so suspicious of Marina today?" Sabine felt quite angry about it.

"I recognize that jewelry box," Mary looked at the box Sabine had placed on the table, seeing how upset Sabine was getting about Marina. "It is the same one your mom kept her charm bracelet in." Mary gestured for permission to pick it up.

"Of course," Sabine pushed the box towards Mary. "I am not even sure how it landed in my glove compartment, but it did."

"Everything that is lost will be found when it needs to be," Mary recited, opening the box. Tears sprung into the old woman's eyes as she saw the bracelet Valarie had had since a young girl. "It is your mother's bracelet," Mary whispered, tears rolling down her weathered cheeks.

"So, it is mom's bracelet?" Sabine moved closer to see it.

Mary turned the small silver baby shoe that hung from it; it had the initials SD on it.

"This was from your father when you were born," Mary wiped at the tears. "If it was found now, it means your mama wants you to have it." Mary handed it to Sabine.

"She always said it would be mine one day," Sabine took the bracelet from Mary. She was about to put it back in the box when Mary stopped her.

"Why don't you try it on?" Mary asked, taking the bracelet and putting it on Sabine's wrist before she could say anything. "There you go. It looks great on you, sweetie."

"I used to love listening to mom tell me the stories behind each charm," Sabine smiled, holding her arm up and admiring the bracelet.

"Now, where were we?" Mary poured them both some more tea, not saying anything about the new charm on the chain. "Ah, that's right; you were going to tell me what was going on?"

"How about you give me a few more Beignets first?" Sabine laughed. For some reason, she felt calm and focused. The sugar from the sweet tea and Beignets must be doing the trick. Sabine thought as she popped another into her mouth.

"NOW, SABINE, BE CAREFUL OUT THERE," Mary said as she walked with Sabine to her SUV. "I wish you would let me come with you, child."

"No, Mary," Sabine moved herself into the driver's seat. "I have already involved you enough by telling you everything."

"Wait," Mary rushed into the house, and then came barreling back out with a treat box in her hand. She opened the passenger door and placed the remainder of the Beignets on her seat. "I know you should not have too much sugar, but you have been up for hours. You need the extra energy."

Mary popped open the glove compartment to put the jewelry box Sabine had left on the table in. Her eyes fell on the daggers, and she drew in her breath.

"Sabine," Mary stood, staring in shock at the daggers. "Please, girl, tell me those are not the daggers you were talking about," Mary said, knowing how stupid that must sound but praying they were somehow fakes or replicas.

"Yes," Sabine said, looking at Mary curiously. "Why?"

Mary said nothing. She flicked her wrist, and Sabine's keys flew out of her hand into Mary's.

"Sorry, Sabine, but I cannot let you go after Kyle and Lydia," Mary started to close the passenger door.

"Mary," Sabine shouted, climbing back out of the car, "What the hell?" Sabine stormed after the plump little woman that moved relatively fast when she wanted to.

Mary disappeared into the house, ignoring Sabine's calls about it getting dark and Marina waiting for her in the library. Before Sabine could storm into the house, Mary came back out dressed in a blue velvet coat and carrying a Mary Poppins type bag.

"What is going on, Mary?" Sabine called as she followed Mary back to the SUV, now thoroughly frustrated and angry because she was losing time.

"You are not going out there on your own," Mary put the box in the back as she got into the passenger seat. "Well, what are you waiting for? Let's go." She clicked the seat belt in place and dropped her bag on her lap.

Sabine shook her head in exasperation. Climbing into the car, she took the keys from Mary.

"Are you going to tell me about those daggers?" Sabine asked Mary as they turned onto the road heading for the office.

"I thought that was what you are going to talk to Marina about?" Mary hugged her bag tightly. She hated being in cars.

"No," Sabine reached into the middle compartment to pull out her phone. She clicked it on; the picture of Elissa was still on the screen. "I wanted to ask her if she knew who this woman was?" she showed Mary.

"Is she the one with the green jewel necklace?" Mary took the phone. "I think I should keep this, and you should keep your attention on the road."

"You are still a nervous passenger, I see," Sabine smiled, noticing Mary gripping her bag with white knuckles.

"There are a bunch idiots on the road," Mary said as if on cue a car zoomed by, making the SUV shake. "Like I said, idiots."

"Yes, that is the woman who goes by the name Elissa," Sabine said. "Don't you think she looks a lot like Amalia?"

"What has Amalia got to do with this?" Mary looked at Sabine, confused.

"Mary," Sabine looked at her, "Amalia is now in charge of the light reapers for our area."

"What?" Mary's brow furrowed. "No, she is not. Odette is holding that position until either you or Lydia take it."

"No," Sabine contradicted her. "Amalia was mom's right-hand person, so she stepped into the position."

"Sabine, dear," Mary turned to look at the girl. "Amalia got fired over a year ago."

"What?" Sabine could not believe what Mary had just said. "You must be mistaken, Mary."

"No, dear, I was there when your mom found out about Amalia's dabbling with the dark arts." Mary was about to tell her more, but the phone rang. It was Amalia.

"Answer it," Mary passed the phone to Sabine, "But pull over first, please," Mary slid the phone to answer.

TEN

Mary's Mysterious Bag

"SABINE?" AMALIA'S VOICE SOUNDED PANICKED AND frantic. "Sabine, are you there?"

Sabine pulled over, and taking the phone from Mary, she put it to her ear.

"Yes, I am here," Sabine answered, keeping her voice calm and steady while her heartbeat quickened in her chest.

If what Mary had said was true? Who else at the office was involved with this? How did Amalia just step back in and take over if she had been fired a year ago?

This was all just getting too much for Sabine.

"Please, Sabine, this crazy woman I thought was an agent has us," Amalia's voice was strained. "She wants her daggers back before ten tonight, or she will kill your aunt and me."

"Is my aunt there with you?" Sabine asked her calmly.

"Yes, she is," Amalia confirmed. "And some angry spirit."

Sabine could not help but smile, her heart quickening knowing Amalia meant Kyle.

"This woman wants his soul." Amalia whispered, "I think she is a dark reaper."

"Where?" Sabine asked; there was something about Amalia's voice that was making her suspicious.

"What?" Amalia was confused by the question.

"Where does she want me to bring the daggers?" Sabine asked.

"The cemetery behind the Old Church restaurant, the Mathews crypt."

Mathews? Sabine felt cold; that was the name the spirit from the cemetery had mentioned to Sabine earlier.

"Okay," Sabine agreed, "but I need assurance my aunt and Kyle are okay."

"I can't do that, Sabine," Amalia whispered hoarsely into the phone. "This crazed demon woman only gave me a few minutes to talk to you."

"I can't bring some ancient daggers to a graveyard that could unleash holy hell without knowing my aunt and Kyle are okay," Sabine said stubbornly. She realized that if the woman wanted the daggers, she needed them for some sort of ritual.

"Sabine, be reasonable. You are playing with my and your aunt's life here," Amalia hissed angrily. "I know the woman needs the knives and your aunt to perform some sort of ritual. So, that is your guarantee that they are still okay. Thanks for caring about me, by the way."

"Okay, I will be there," Sabine hung up and put the phone back into the middle compartment. She sat there for a few minutes staring off into the sunset.

"Sabine?" Mary rubbed Sabine's back and felt her tension, fear, and apprehension there.

"What am I doing, Mary?" Sabine put her head onto her steering wheel. "I am not cut out for all this cloak and dagger shit." She was surrounded by actual cloaks and daggers.

"Remember when you were little? You loved to play hide and seek." Mary smiled as Sabine turned her head to look at her. "You were always the one that needed to seek rather than hide."

"Really?" Sabine wondered why she had not remembered that. "I used to love to look for people?"

"Oh, yes," Mary laughed. "And you were so good at finding people. No one could hide from you."

"Oh?" Sabine sat up, fascinated by Mary's story.

"Yes, that is when your mother discovered one of your many gifts," Mary smiled at her. "You would scooch down on the ground, close your eyes, and somehow feel where they had gone."

"I did?" Sabine's mind flashed to the cemetery when she had instinctively known how to communicate with the lost souls and find the ones that would help her with Tatum.

"You have gifts, Sabine, that you have not tapped into yet," Mary told her encouragingly.

"Gifts?" Sabine asked skeptically. "I think my powers are more of a curse, Mary," Sabine said as she started the car. They still needed to get to the library as Sabine needed to know who or what she was up against to free her aunt and help Kyle.

"Why do you say that, child?" Mary asked her, shocked.

"Well, my whole life, mom and dad, even you, have covered them up or cloaked them." Sabine's hand automatically went to her neck. "You all told me not to ever show anyone what I could do. Mom even wrote a spell I recite each night to ensure I don't go too deeply into my dreams."

"Sabine," Mary touched Sabine's arm gently, her heart heavy that she would think they wanted her to ever be less than she was. "None of us ever wanted to stifle your powers."

"It never seemed that way to me," Sabine said sadly as she pulled up in front of the office. "I am going to run in quick." Sabine slid out of the car.

"Okay. I will wait here then," Mary waved Sabine off. She needed to get a look at the cloak lying on the back seat.

/ / /

"YOU ARE SUCH A TWO-FACED SLIMY WEASEL," Kyle yelled. "Just you wait, you are going to be very, very sorry you ever double-crossed Sabine."

"Keep your voice down," Tatum ordered Kyle. "You need to help me wake Lydia up."

"How do you propose I do that?" Kyle held up his ghostly hand and swung a fist that went right through Tatum's pompous head. Kyle stood back, amazed. Tatum had flinched when Kyle had run his hand through his head.

"Stop messing around and put your ghostly mitts to good use," Tatum hissed at him. "Concentrate on centering the cold air around you, then place your hands on either side of Lydia's temples."

"Oh, noooo," Kyle backed away. "For all I know, you are trying to get me to kill her and then frame me for it in front of Sabine."

"Don't be so melodramatic, you dumb spirit," Tatum shook his head. "Now, either help me with this, or I will see to it that you go back into the infinity fire cuffs."

"It was you!" Kyle glared at the man with his perfect hair and Don Juan type smile. "You did that to me."

"Look, I do not have time to sit here and argue with a damn ghost," Tatum said, getting angry now. "So, either do this or go back into the infinity fire, your choice," he looked at Kyle coldly.

"Fine, but so help me, if anything happens to Lydia or Sabine …" Kyle glared at Tatum angrily.

"You will what?" Tatum shrugged at him. "Haunt me for the rest of my life?" Tatum gave him a nasty smile. "Do you even know what is being prepared for you out there right now?"

"Do I want to know?" Kyle shuddered. He may only be energy right now, but his energy was more in tune with his instincts than he had ever been alive.

"No, you don't," Tatum told him cruelly. "Now, do what I have asked and wake her up."

Kyle cupped Lydia's head with his hands and concentrated. He could feel the cold rise up from the earth and flow through him like he was a funnel. The cold shot from his spirit fingers and jolted Lydia from her spell induced trance.

Lydia's eyes focused on Kyle. "You again," Lydia said, trying to sit up. Kyle automatically went to help her and passed right through her. "Stop that," Lydia moaned as the ice-cold slid through her.

"I am so sorry, Lydia," Kyle said. "But that baff…" Before he could finish his sentence, he was sucked away.

"I AM SORRY, Sabine, but I have never seen that woman before in my life," Marina held Sabine's phone, her thick glasses sitting on her nose. "She is not in the client or the agent files, either."

"Okay, thanks, Marina," Sabine hugged the small woman. Something felt different about Marina. "Are you okay?"

"Yes, I am fine," Marina gave Sabine a strange look. "Why do you ask?"

"No reason; was just wondering," Sabine frowned. "Well, I had best be going to find Kyle and Lydia."

"Is Lydia missing?" Marina looked at Sabine, startled. "Is she okay?"

That was weird? Sabine thought. Sabine and Kyle had sought her help only that morning right after discovering that her aunt had been taken. Sabine stared at Marina. Was she losing her mind? Sabine knew she had taken the death of her mom badly as they had been more like sisters. Marina had grown up in Lydia and Hayden's home as she was orphaned at a young age. That must be it. Sabine thought.

"No, they are fine," Sabine would have a word with Robert on her way out. "I must go. Mary is waiting for me in the car."

"Okay, Sabine. It was really good to see you again. You must stop by more often," Marina blew Sabine a kiss as she always had done when Sabine had left.

Something was not right here! Sabine hurried over to Robert.

"Hello, little miss Sabine," Robert greeted her with a smile. "What can I do for you?"

"Was I here earlier today?" Sabine asked Robert, getting a curious look from him.

"Why yes, you were with your friend in spirit wearing some sort of cloak," Robert frowned. "Not sure why you would want to bring such darkness here, but we let you through because of who your mama was."

"I came to see Marina and Amalia," Sabine told Robert.

"Marina?" Robert looked at her, his brow crinkling. "She has not been in for almost three months now. She took your mama's death hard and eventually had a breakdown. She has been on bereavement leave ever since. She came back this afternoon."

"What about Amalia?" Sabine asked Robert, a little alarmed by the news about Marina.

"Not sure why that woman was ever allowed back in this building," Robert made a disgusted face. "But she was asked to stand in for Odette, who went on maternity leave four months ago."

"Robert, when last did you see Amalia?" Sabine asked Robert.

"This afternoon. She came to collect those books from your mama," Robert told her. "I had to carry the box out to her car."

"Why would she take my mother's books?" Sabine asked him.

"Not all of them, just the three big ones on the Ancient dark arts," Robert told Sabine.

"Thanks, Robert," Sabine hugged the giant. "You have been a great …"

A scream came from Sabine's car. Both Robert and Sabine rushed to the SUV. The cloak was swirling around Mary, who was trying to beat it off with some kind of gold and blue pole. Sabine and Robert looked at each in shock. Sabine reached for the passenger door while Robert ran around to the driver's side. The doors would not open. Sabine clicked the remote on the key, but nothing happened.

"Sabine, look in …" the cloak swirled around her and disappeared, taking Mary with it.

"Mary," Sabine screamed, yanking on the door handle so hard that Sabine flew back when it opened. She would have landed on the sidewalk if she had not been hanging onto the door handle.

"I told you …" Robert said as he climbed into the car to look around. "Dark magic."

⁄⁄⁄

MARY GOT DUMPED into what looked like some sort of tomb.

"What the bejesus lady," Kyle yelled, "You nearly scared me half to death."

"Ah," Mary said, "I see I have made my way to the right place then. And I hate to break this to you son, but you are already dead."

"Mary?" Lydia asked, getting up to hug the woman who had practically raised her. "What on earth are you doing here?" Lydia shook her.

"Leading the way for Sabine," Mary shrugged. "You must be Kyle."

"Yes, and I hear you know Sabine?" Kyle was eager to ask Mary about Sabine.

"Calm down, lad," Mary felt the man's anxiety about Sabine.

What a pity he had to go get himself cursed and dead to discover his heart, Mary thought. She felt sad for Sabine as well. These two would have been good for each other.

"Sabine is going to be fine now. She is a bit anxious to find you two," Mary told them.

"She is going to be fine?" Lydia asked Mary. "What did you do?"

"Oh, nothing. Just got rid of a spy. A spy that was also cloaking her ability to see what was right in front of her." Mary brandished the gold and blue walking stick she had in her hand, and the now deactivated black cloak appeared.

"The cloak?" Kyle said. "I thought it helped Sabine. It helped to disguise me. It even granted me twenty minutes of being human again to help Sabine."

"What do you mean?" Lydia and Mary said at the same time, their full attention now turned to Kyle.

///

"WHERE DID THAT THING TAKE MARY?" Sabine was getting a bit tired of people being sucked out of her car.

"I think you should be asking where Mary made that thing take her," Robert suggested. "I know Miss Mary. Ain't no dark object ever got the better of her."

"Really?" Sabine looked at Robert.

"Where do you think your mama, Miss Marina, and Miss Lydia learned all that stuff they know about the dark arts?" Robert finished looking around Sabine's car. He was making sure there were no dark magic or spelled items left behind. He handed Sabine Mary's bag. "I think she wanted you to have this for some reason. I know this because Miss Mary never leaves this thing behind."

"Thank you, Robert," Sabine stood on the pavement, clutching Mary's giant handbag.

"I must be on my way, Miss Sabine. That's if you are okay now." Robert smiled at her.

"I am fine. Thank you for helping me, Robert."

Sabine stood, staring at the empty car seat where Mary had been. That is the third person she had lost today.

Sabine walked around the car and climbed into the

driver's seat. She felt like she had moved into her car, having spent most of the day in it. As she started the ignition, she looked at the gas level. She would have to fill the tank soon. Right now though, she had to try and figure out a game plan for the cemetery. Sabine moved into the traffic and headed for her favorite spot to get a decent coffee, a great bagel, and sort out her thoughts.

She turned into the parking lot of the outdoor ice rink. She loved to park here, watch people skate, and have a good cup of coffee. It always helped her unwind, especially when some professional skaters took to the ice to practice. Sabine got out of her car and walked over to the kiosk.

"Hey Sabine," Jessie gave her a warm smile. "Do you want your usual?"

"Hi Jessie," Sabine smiled back. "Yes, please."

Jessie popped into the back and returned within a few minutes, handing Sabine a steaming coffee cup and a fresh warm bagel with cream cheese.

"Thanks, Jessie." Sabine handed over the money and took the goodies. "Have a good night."

"You too, Sabine," Jessie called after her.

Sabine got back into her car and locked the doors. Something she never did, but for some reason tonight, it made her feel safer. She balanced her coffee and bagel on the dashboard while she pulled on her jacket; the evening was cooling down the air. As she was about to pick up her bagel, Mary's bag started to jerk. At first, Sabine thought there was a small animal in it.

Clearly, she would have felt if there was an animal in the bag? Sabine thought.

Maybe it was just her mind playing tricks on her. It had been a long day, but the bag jerked again. The bag was definitely jerking.

Sabine looked at it. Reaching for it like it was something you had to do but didn't want to, like when she had to help a house snake stuck in some plastic. Sabine shuddered at that memory. She hated snakes. That memory brought back another one. A memory of her childhood friend. Sabine could not remember his name, only that he was the boy in the mirror.

Sabine smiled as she remembered dragging the mirror all over with her. Like her, he came from a preternatural family and was also isolated from other kids. Their families were old-time friends; they had spelled two mirrors so the kids could play together and become friends.

Whatever happened to that mirror or their friendship? Sabine could not remember it was a long time ago. She shook the memory off and went back to find out what was in Mary's mysterious jiggling bag.

"Okay, bag, if there is a snake in there, I will be very angry." Sabine pointed at it as if it was a naughty child, "Now I am going to open you and take a peek; please don't let anything jump out at me. I never liked the Jack-in-the-box." Good grief; I am talking to a bag.

"Well, here goes," Sabine popped open the latch. Holding the bag a safe distance away, she opened it up, instinctively leaning back as she did. "There is nothing in here."

That was weird. Sabine put her hand in the bag with the black lining and felt around — nothing. She picked it up, flipped it over and shook, some pages, paper-clipped together, tumbled out. Okay, it was official: her Mary was Mary Poppins.

Sabine closed the clasped on the bag, "We would not want anything else magically tumbling out you now, would we?" She said to the bag and gently placed it on the seat, leaned over, and strapped it in with the safety belt. "There you go." She patted it.

Sabine picked up the pages; they were the spelled pages from her mother's book she had seen that morning in the library. The book on ancient arts of magic and the origins of demons.

Why would these pages be spelled, and why were they in Mary's bag? Curious, Sabine reached for her coffee; she took a swallow and took the paper clip off. She was about to turn a page when the top pages peeled off and flew onto the floor. Leaving only a few pages in her hands.

"Rude," Sabine said, looking at the bag as if it had done it.

She looked down at the pages in her hand and froze. The page was titled The Tale of Six Daggers. Down each margin was a drawing of six ancient daggers. Daggers that each had a different color jeweled handle. Two of the daggers in the pictures looked identical to the ones in Sabine's glove compartment. The others were similar but had a green, blue, black, and clear crystal handle. The one with the clear crystal looked different from the other five.

ELEVEN

A Tale of Six Daggers

SABINE GLANCED AT THE CLOCK ON HER DASHBOARD. SHE still had three hours to spare before she took the daggers to the cemetery. She had time to read the six daggers' story, a story that Mary had obviously wanted her to read. The story may shed some light on what was going on and why Elissa wanted the daggers. It may even answer some questions about Amalia and why she had lied to Sabine about being kidnapped. Robert's timeline for Amalia's did not match the one Amalia had about being taken.

So much for a nice simple, quiet life. Sabine sighed and caught a look at her nails. She had to stop biting her nails.

Sabine knew she should delve right into the story she held in her hands while all she wanted to do was pull a blanket over her head and wish that everything would go away. She was not cut out for all this mystery stuff, the lies, deceit, and all that went with magic, powers, and this life. It was why she had left it in the first place.

Sabine's eyes drifted to her wrist. One of the charms on her mother's bracelet caught her eye. Sabine could not remember that charm being on the bracelet. She held it up to the light. It was a small silver mirror, identical to the one she had as a kid. That was probably the reason Sabine had thought about the boy in the mirror.

Sabine glanced at the clock again. The time was ticking by slowly. She did not know if she was glad about it or if she just wanted to get whatever was going to happen over with.

Sabine saw the bag jiggle again from the corner of her eye, and the papers flapped.

"Okay, okay," Sabine said to the bag. "It is like living in the Beast's enchanted castle with talking teacups and candlesticks."

Sabine switched the two front interior lights on, sat back, and started to read. Many of the words were written in an ancient script that her mother had tried to teach her. But, old forgotten languages were not Sabine's thing. The weird symbols stuck between jumbled words were like crossword puzzles to Sabine, and she hated puzzles. But, some of the pages were in English, and she was able to read them. The section she could understand was about Nocheli, a reaper that to Sabine's kind was like the boogeyman to humans.

THE TALE OF NOCHELI and the Origins of the 5 Demon Daggers

Nocheli was the first watcher to question her destiny. She was also the first watcher to reject her life mate. She had been born different from the other watchers. All watchers were born under the soothing light of a silver moon. But Nocheli's mother had experienced complications, and she was born under the light of the sun. At first, the high reapers had said she was a gift from the golden light and allowed her to exist.

Nocheli was not born evil; she was born of the golden light, which was meant to shine upon the world and encourage change and growth. But change is not something any being has ever taken lightly, especially the Preternatural such as the watchers, demons, and magical beings.

Nocheli tried to live her life and give her four children born of Ray, the human she fell in love with, and whom she eloped with, a good life, even though the Council of Watchers had driven Ray insane. They had doomed his soul to be tortured by the dark reapers and warped his mind, rendering him an invalid. This was a consequence of Nocheli's betrayal and breaking the ancient protocols of the high reapers.

Through everything Nocheli was forced to endure, she remained faithful to the light that shone through her soul. But, through the betrayal of all those she loved, including Ray, her children, and the communities that had taken them, the light was dulled. Nocheli's darkness was born because of the light. She sacrificed her soul to save those she loved, so they could live in the light. But even in darkness, Nocheli never tipped the delicate balance of the universe.

Tempted by the allure of immortality, never aging, and a life of abundance, Nocheli's children joined their father and aligned with the demon known as The Darkness. However, every contract with a demon comes with a price. For The Darkness, it was souls. To gain immortality and youthfulness. They needed to feed The Darkness souls. As they were part reaper, Nocheli's children could reap souls.

Wanting her children to experience a normal childhood that she never had, Nocheli had four jewels made, one for each of her children. They were magic jewels that both blocked and trapped any inhuman powers her children may have. They were worn as amulets by each of her four children.

When Nocheli's children tricked her into forging them each a soul dagger, Nocheli did so, glad that her children had chosen to follow the watchers' ways. No longer needing their jeweled amulets, Nocheli placed the jewels in the hilt of each dagger.

To help her husband Ray, Nocheli forged him a dagger, topped with an onyx. Only his dagger was not for reaping but to house his soul and ease the endless torture. Nocheli had to take his place to get Ray's soul back, not as a tortured soul but a dark reaper. Nocheli's dagger had been forged of the purest gold with a crystal-clear diamond, a gift of the sun, moon, earth, and night.

Watchers are reapers that don't choose between the two sects; they remain neutral. Their daggers were only ever used to free a trapped soul or to assist a reaper, no matter which side of the veil the reaper was from. But Nocheli was forced to choose a side to protect her children, village, and husband from the watchers' wrath. Only the dark reapers came to her aide.

Nocheli's defection not only birthed a new breed of demon, but it also caused a war between the watchers, the dark, and the light reapers. As hard as Nocheli had tried not to tip the balance, she had. This war allowed The Darkness to escape and create a new kind of soul reaper, one that did not only reap the souls of the dead. The five daggers Nocheli had forged her family became known as the demon daggers.

/ / /

THE REST of the text was written in the language Sabine could not read, mixed with English words that looked like they had been redacted.

"No, no, no," Sabine held the pages up to the light. Why would it be redacted? Sabine turned and glared at the bag.

"Did you do this?" She asked the bag crossly. The bag just sat there safely belted-in on the seat. Sabine had learned something new about Nocheli, the mother of The Darkness, as they called her, but not enough, or what she needed to know.

Sabine still did not know why she would feel a trapped soul's anguish whenever she touched the daggers' handle. Or what the heck that Elissa woman or even Amalia was doing with them.

This day just brought more and more questions with very little to no answers. Sabine fished the daggers out of the glove compartment. She was careful to grip them by the blade so she could hold the jewels up to the light. Something inside the jewels swirled and twirled; Sabine shivered. Wondering if a soul might have been trapped in there.

Sabine picked up her phone and scrolled through to the picture of Elissa. The picture and profile were gone.

"Shoot," Sabine swore, then rifled through the pages to find the one with the drawing of the daggers.

There was the amber one and the red one. They were an exact match to the two she had. Was the green jewel Elissa had worn from the green dagger? Another thought struck Sabine, so she phoned Marina, hoping to get the real Marina this time.

"Sabine?" Marina answered. "Are you alright?"

"Yes, why do you ask?" Sabine frowned, chewing her nails.

"It's just after half-past nine," Marina yawned.

"Oh, shoot. Sorry, did I wake you?" Sabine had been so absorbed in Nocheli's story. She did not realize the time.

"It's okay," Marina assured her. "Do you need something?"

"Yes," Sabine asked her if she knew anything about Nocheli and her children.

While Marina told Sabine what she knew about Nocheli, her children, and the demon daggers, Sabine put her phone on Bluetooth. She listened intently to Marina as she drove towards the Old Church cemetery.

///

THE CEMETERY WAS dark except for the low glow of the lantern-style lights dotted along the graves' neat rows. Sabine nibbled nervously on her nails while she sat in the graveyard parking lot as Marina finished her story.

"Sabine?" Marina called. "Are you still there, or have I been speaking to myself this whole time?"

"I'm still here." Unfortunately, Sabine thought. "Thank you. This is all helpful to know."

"Sabine, are you sure everything is alright?" Marina's voice was full of concern. "Are you in your car?"

"Yes," Sabine answered. "And yes. I have an assignment."

"At this time of night?" Marina asked.

"Marina, while you were away, did you have anyone filling in for you?" Sabine asked, deliberately ignoring Marina's question.

"Yes, Amalia brought in one of her sisters," Marina's voice held a twinge of anger. "I never needed to go on leave. I was forced. Just like poor Odette, who wanted to work up until her fourth trimester."

"Do you know what her sister's name was?" Sabine asked, a feeling of trepidation crawling up her spine.

"Uh, Elizabeth, Ellie …" Marina thought. "No, it was Eliza."

"Who brought Amalia back into the office as I thought she was fired?" Sabine asked Marina.

"Some new hotshot from the Council. I believe he is one of the council member's sons and on their protocol investigations and enforcement team," Marina got angrier as she spoke. "I believe he's friends with Amalia or one of her sisters," Marina lashed. "Apparently, they are now after him for some or other reason, though. I say good riddance. At least, Odette and I have our positions back."

"Do you know what his name is?" Sabine asked.

"No, sorry, Sabine, I don't. But I could find out for you tomorrow if you want me to." Marina offered.

"No, don't worry," Sabine breathed. She had a pretty good idea of what his name was. "One last thing …" Sabine asked Marina if shapeshifters existed and was not sure she was happy with the answer.

After once again apologizing for waking Marina, Sabine hung up the phone. She closed her eyes and breathed. Well, that was just great then.

Not only was she walking into a trap set by two or three deranged sisters, but they were sisters who could alter a person's perception of what they looked like. To top it all, they had the help of a powerful warlock who could mesmerize people.

She had procrastinated in the car long enough. It was time to go face down whatever was waiting for her in the dead of night in the graveyard. Sabine took the two daggers and went around to the trunk of her car. She opened it, pulled down a hidden compartment in the back seats, and took out a cloth. She wrapped up the daggers in the fabric, clipped on her knife belt, then reached for her soul dagger, sheathing it in its pocket behind her back. Sabine slipped off her cardigan and shrugged into her leather jacket, which hung down to her mid-thigh. She scooped her long hair back into a ponytail.

She took a deep breath, closed the trunk, and then walked to the entrance gate.

Now, all I need are some cool shades and wicked Kung Fu skills! Sabine thought. Clutching the cloth in her hands, she dug out her mobile phone and switched on the light.

Graveyards should have floodlights, not low-lit lights. Sabine shuddered.

Sabine looked at the clock on her phone. She still had fifteen minutes to find the Mathews crypt. She drew her jacked together and walked into the cemetery, like one of those stupid people in a scary movie you usually screamed at.

TWELVE

Sabine versus the Soul Eaters

SABINE HAD DEALT WITH SPIRITS HER WHOLE LIFE. SHE knew not to fear them. Well, most of them. And she could communicate with them. But she still did not like being in a cemetery at night. That was just looking for trouble and not from the spirits either.

Sabine shuddered as the night birds made their horrible, morbid noise. As if on cue, a tall yellow-legged night bird ran across the path in front of her, scaring the heck out of Sabine.

"You stupid bird," Sabine hissed at it.

She wished there was some sort of app that would guide you to a grave as she stumbled through the yard looking for the Mathews crypt.

"Did it have to be a freaking crypt?" Sabine muttered.

Sabine.

A whisper floated to her. She jumped and turned around; holding out her phone like one would a knife. Around her, the trees' leaves fluttered as a gentle breeze picked up.

She was going to need a psych ward after this if her

heart did not give out first. Her heart was trying to hammer its way through her chest. She hoped that Mr. Smooth, the double-crossing psycho warlock, had hiked home by now. She did not want to have to deal with him ...

"Hello again, Sabine," a familiar voice drifted to her from behind.

Dang and she did not even have to say his name three times! Sabine closed her eyes. Please, let me be hearing things. Please, let me be hearing things.

Sabine was not sure if she was praying or chanting but hoped he was another figment of her imagination or merely a voice in her head.

Sabine ... Sabine...

The whispers got louder. She shook her head, trying to block out all the sounds she was hearing.

"I am not going to go away, Sabine," Tatum drawled.

Nope. He was still there behind me. He was no voice in my head, but an angry corporeal warlock.

Sabine pursed her lips and slowly turned around, her mobile phone at the ready.

"Are you going to stab me with your phone, or do you want me to make a call for you?" Tatum asked with raised eyebrows.

Well, at least he looked amused. That was good, right? He did not seem angry that she had sicced some spirits on him.

"Have you been here the entire afternoon, or have you just arrived?" Sabine asked him, still holding her mobile phone out defensively.

"I should be mad at you for running out on me and leaving me stranded with no way home," Tatum told her. "I should be doubly mad at you for that little stunt you pulled. What are you, a ghost whisperer?"

"I know a lot of people, both dead and alive," Sabine shrugged. "What are you doing here, Tatum?" Sabine more than likely knew the answer to that, but she needed to keep him talking to figure out her next escape plan.

"I came looking for you," he told her, his eyes dropping the cloth in her hand.

"I am sure you did," Sabine told him. "Look, I have something to do right now and don't have time to stand here, talking about your monstrous deeds."

"I am sure you do, and you still do not know what you are talking about," Tatum told her. "And I am coming with you."

"Why?" Sabine asked him. There was a movement behind Tatum that caught Sabine's eye.

"I am here to help you …" Tatum collapsed on the ground, a stunned look on his face.

"Marina!" Sabine could not believe Marina was standing there. If it was Marina, that is? Sabine eyed the woman suspiciously.

"Quick, this way," Marina beckoned to Sabine. "Why on earth would you be running around a graveyard at this time of night?"

"I am visiting a relative," Sabine told Marina, almost certain the woman was a shapeshifter. Not her Marina.

Sabine …

The whispers called to her again. She stopped, tilted her head, and listened to what the spirits were trying to tell her.

"What is it, Sabine?" Marina asked. "Is someone coming?" Marina looked around nervously.

"What are you doing here, Marina?" Sabine asked.

"I should be asking you what you are doing creeping around a graveyard at night," Marina said. "Didn't your mother teach you anything?

"Actually," Sabine was about to grab her dagger when a voice drifted to them.

"She knows," Tatum walked up to where the imposter Marina stood, rubbing his head where he had been whacked. "You did not have to whack me that hard," he groaned.

"Eliza, I take it?" Sabine said to the woman wearing Marina's face.

"Correct," Eliza morphed back to her form.

She was not what Sabine expected. Like Tatum, she had jet black hair.

"Why pretend to be Marina?" Sabine asked instinctively, gripping the daggers tighter and taking a step back.

"You ask way too many questions," Eliza told her. "I see you are not wearing your cloak, Sabine?"

"It's a bit too nippy to wear a cloak tonight," Sabine took a step back, following the whispers.

"Come now, Sabine, there is nowhere for you to run," Tatum watched her trying to inch away. "Your friends in the graveyard, the dead ones, they won't be helping you tonight."

"No, they don't want to become food," Eliza and Tatum looked at each laughing.

That was her cue. She turned and ran following the directions of the whispers. She hoped to hell her ghostly GPS knew what they were doing. As she ran, she heard Eliza and Tatum calling after her. Nearing the towering statue of Nocheli, Sabine heard the sounds of someone chanting in a voice that sounded like her aunt's.

Sabine ducked behind a gravestone, carefully making her way nearer to where she could see a blonde woman leaning on her hands and knees over a body. She could also hear the familiar sound of Kyle shouting as he cussed at the woman, and then yelled for Lydia and Mary to snap out of it. Relief and fear flooded Sabine at the same time. All three of them were there together.

Sabine crept a little closer. Her aunt was in a trance-like state. She chanted on her knees next to the grave beneath the statue of Nocheli. Mary had been bound and gagged on the opposite side of the grave to Lydia, while Kyle's wrists blazed with the infinity fire at the foot of the grave.

Kyle's body lay on top of the disturbed soil of the grave. Not looking where she was crouching, she crunched some dry leaves, catching Kyle's attention. And just like Kyle, who could not shut up, yelled.

"Help me," Kyle shouted. "This crazy lady is trying to eat my soul."

The woman pinning down Kyle's hands and legs turned towards the noise of the leaves.

"Amalia?" Sabine stared in shock.

"Sabine?" Amalia looked surprised to see her.

Amalia jumped up and onto the side of the grave. She looked as if she had been caught with her hand in the cookie jar. Or, in this case, the soul jar.

"You are not supposed to be here," Amalia looked towards the cemetery entrance.

"Where am I supposed to be?" Sabine asked, keeping the tombstone between her and Amalia.

Sabine could not believe this woman with the crazed eyes was the same immaculate, prim, and proper Amalia she knew.

"Where are the others?" Amalia ignored her question.

"What are you doing, Amalia?" Sabine asked her.

"I am a soul eater; to prolong my life and maintain my powers, I have to eat fresh souls." Amalia flicked her wrist, and Kyle buckled, screaming in pain. "But you already knew or suspected as much."

"Stop. You are hurting him," Sabine tried to rush to Kyle, but Amalia stood in her way and looked at Sabine with cold eyes.

"You're too late. Your aunt has nearly finished the ritual." Amalia gave Sabine an evil smile.

Sabine looked at Kyle's body, sprawled out in the dirt. The green jeweled dagger protruded from his heart.

"The green jewel is yours?" Sabine asked, watching her closely.

"Yes, it is mine," Amalia confirmed.

"Then why did you give me the amber one to reap Kyle's soul?" Sabine asked.

"I did not give it to you. My sister gave you the wrong dagger," Amalia explained. "As Elissa had been seeing Kyle, he thought it had been her with him that night."

"It was you who cursed Kyle?" Sabine took a step closer to the grave.

Amalia looked behind her. She sidestepped Sabine but was careful not to step on the grave as she blocked the path to Kyle's spirit.

"My sister could not make it that night. She was off on an important mission. So, I stood in for her," Amalia gave Sabine a cruel smile. She could feel the jealousy and anger building in Sabine. Amalia now knew for sure Sabine had developed feelings for her target.

"That is why the knife did not work on Kyle. It was your mark that had cursed him. So, only the green dagger could reap his soul for you." Sabine figured out loud.

"Sabine, can you forgo the twenty questions and take her out already?" Kyle shouted, the pain tearing through his soul.

Amalia waved her wrist again, silencing Kyle.

"Well, look at you, finally figuring it out," Amalia told her nastily. "Now, stand back so I can finish what I started." Amalia turned, clicked her fingers as Lydia started chanting, and Kyle's voice returned. His screams of agony made Amalia create a face like she was eating something delicious.

"Aunt Lydia," Sabine yelled, but her aunt could not hear her, and Amalia once again took up her position on top of Kyle's body.

"Sabine, do your thing," Kyle screamed, buckling at the agony Amalia was causing.

"Kyle," Sabine ran to him, but she could not touch him, and the infinity fire singed her flesh.

"Sabine," Kyle called again, the pain burning through his soul like he was being cooked on a barbeque pit.

Sabine stood her eyes going from her aunt to Kyle and then to Mary. How did she save them?

Sabine ran towards Mary, who struggled against her magic bonds, but she could not pull her free. Mary gestured with her eyes to something behind her. Sabine fumbled around, and Mary's cane appeared. Sabine did not know if she needed to wave it like a fairy Godmother or bash Amalia with it.

Sabine decided to bash Amalia with it. Turning, she rushed at the crazed soul eater and swung Mary's cane like a baseball bat. The cane connected with Amalia, and it knocked her screeching through the air, then she thudded to the ground. The minute Amalia hit the dirt, her aunt, Mary, and Kyle were released from the hold she had on them.

"Nice swing, Sabine girl," Mary told Sabine, then took the cane from her. "But I think I will take that now."

"Sabine," Lydia rushed over to her niece and hugged her. "Where is Kyle?" She looked around frantically. "I am so sorry," Lydia said to the grumbling ghost appearing next to them.

"Did you kill her?" Kyle asked, looking towards Amalia's body, lying in a heap.

"I am not sure," Sabine looked over at Amalia.

"Sabine," two other angry voices rushed towards them, stopping at the foot of the grave.

"We have been looking for you," Tatum told her, looking at all of them standing together like they were cattle about to be slaughtered.

"Amalia," a woman Sabine had not seen before rushed to Amalia's side.

"Elissa, I presume?" Sabine said softly, and the trio with her nodded.

"Nasty piece of work that one," Mary whispered. "She has the siren tongue. Do not let her draw you in."

"Good to know," Sabine nodded. "Tatum can mesmerize. This just keeps getting better."

"Here, you gave me this when you went to play baseball with Amalia," Mary gave Sabine the cloth with the daggers in.

"What did you do to Amalia?" Eliza hissed at Sabine. "She is going to make you pay for that," Eliza said with relish.

Elissa helped Amalia up, and Tatum had a look at the wound on her head from hitting the gravestone. At the same time, Eliza did some hocus pocus on Amalia's lump, where Sabine had hit her with the cane.

"Can you hear that?" Kyle asked quietly, looking around. "I could swear I heard someone calling to us, Sabine."

"Yes, I did hear something," Sabine whispered back to Kyle, amazed that he had heard the calling too. "I think it is coming from this grave." All four of them looked down. They were about to jump off the grave, but Sabine stopped them.

"It is disrespectful to stand on someone's grave," Mary whispered to Sabine.

"I know, but this is not just one grave," Sabine tilted her head as the whispering grew louder. "I think it is a mass grave of not only bodies but trapped souls."

"Then I say we hop off it this instant," Mary was about to, but Lydia grabbed her.

"No, Mary, listen to Sabine and Kyle," Lydia told her. "I feel the souls want us here."

"They are all like me," Kyle looked startled as he heard the voices. "This is like Amalia's food cupboard." His eyes were huge with shock.

"All the more reason to get off, I say," Mary tried to pull out of Lydia's grip.

"No, Mary," Sabine said. An image of Tatum's side-stepping the grave earlier that day flashed through her head. Then she thought about how cautious Amalia was not to actually stand on the grave or touch the ground. "I don't think the four soul-stealing demons over there can step on the grave."

"So, why store souls beneath it?" Kyle asked. "If she eats souls, why not just consume them all at once? Are they leftovers, maybe?"

"Kyle, do you think you can get down there?" Sabine asked him.

"Down there, as in the grave?" Kyle asked her in disbelief. "I don't like dark closed-up places, and being buried alive is a bad nightmare of mine."

"Kyle, you are already dead, son," Mary told him again. "You can't get stuck down there."

"Tell that to the souls stuck down there," Kyle told Mary. "Fine, I will take a stab at it."

While Kyle tried to disappear into the grave, Mary, Sabine, and Lydia formed a barrier around Kyle's body.

"That was not very nice of you, Sabine." Amalia hissed, advancing on Sabine, only to stop at the edge of the grave. "What the hell did you hit me with?"

"Mary's cane," Sabine told her, watching as Amalia looked behind Sabine towards Mary.

"What cane?" Amalia asked Sabine. She could not see a cane in Mary's hand.

Sabine turned, and the first thing she noticed was that Mary had her blue velvet coat back on, and her cane was missing.

"Where is your cane, Mary?" Sabine asked her beneath her breath.

"I have put it away," Mary smiled sweetly at Sabine.

Mary moved, and the coat fell open, revealing the gold lining. That was when Sabine realized where the cane had gone. Both Mary's coat and bag were magic.

Mary Poppins had nothing on this Mary. Sabine smiled when Mary winked at her.

"Where is Kyle?" Amalia asked, trying to peek through the wall they had formed around the body.

"Why don't you come and see for yourself?" Sabine invited Amalia.

"So, you can hit me with whatever it was you hit me with again?" Amalia asked. "I don't think so."

Tatum, Eliza, and Elissa surrounded the grave with Amalia. They raised their hands, chanting together, a blue light flittered up from the ground forming a barrier around the grave.

"Sabine, we don't have time to stand here and play games with you the whole night," Tatum moved forward. "I need you to give me the daggers and let Amalia finish the ritual. Time is running out for your friend, and you know what happens to cursed souls."

"Where is the green jewel you wore as a necklace?" Sabine ignored Tatum to ask Amalia.

"It was not a necklace. It was spelled to look like one," Amalia explained. "The green jewel sticks out well past the sheath that hangs around our necks." Amalia tugged on the gold chain hanging around her neck. At the end of the chain was a leather sheath. The sheath had markings on it, resembling the markings on the daggers and was just as old. What Amalia said made sense as the daggers were not much bigger than a letter opener, only deadlier and a lot sharper.

Sabine looked at the other three; they all had similar chains around their necks. The only one that had a dagger in it was Eliza's.

"Why do you wear the daggers around your necks like that?" Sabine asked. "It must be very uncomfortable."

"Enough chit-chat," Elissa stepped up to the edge of the grave. "We have a ceremony to complete and three more to do. Time is of the essence." She looked up at the moon.

"Kyle said you were trying to find my mother's grimoire?" Sabine ignored Elissa and turned to Eliza. "How did you manage to use the all-seeing-eye?"

"It was not the all-seeing eye," Eliza lifted her hand over her ring. "It was the evil eye. Even it could not find where your mother hid that thing."

"You put an evil eye around my neck?" Sabine looked at the foolish woman. "That was careless of you."

"Yes, you killed that evil-eye," Eliza glared at her. "Speaking of evil eyes, where is the cloak I gave you?"

"Not sure. It fought with Mary and then kidnapped her," Sabine told Eliza.

"Is that how you got into the crypt?" Eliza glared at Mary. "Lydia said she summoned you."

"No, that dark thing brought me here," Mary confirmed. "I think it is still there."

"It had better be. We need it for tonight," Eliza stormed off to go find the cloak.

"I need to get that blue dagger," Sabine hissed at Mary.

"You mean this dagger?" Kyle's voice came from behind them and in his ghostly hand was the blue jeweled dagger.

"How?" Sabine turned around to look at him, amazed, and took the dagger, adding it to the cloth.

"Turns out I can touch certain dark objects like the daggers and the cloak," Kyle smiled as he looked towards Amalia and Elissa whispering at the grave's edge.

"What about the souls trapped in the grave below us?" Lydia asked before Sabine or Mary could.

"There are three of them," Kyle told them, unsure how to tell Sabine the next part. "They were all reaped over the past week."

"Did they give you their names?" Sabine asked, feeling a massive weight settle in her chest.

"I don't think that is important, Sabine," Kyle told her softly. "I think we should all get the hell out of this cemetery as quick as possible. Don't worry about my body or my new buddies down below. As long as we have the daggers, they cannot touch any of us."

"We can't. The soul suckers have trapped us here." Sabine touched the barrier, and a shock sparked up her arm.

"What did you do with the cloak, old hag?" Eliza stepped up to the side of the grave, her eyes flashing angrily.

"Mary killed that evil thing," Kyle hovered next to Mary, no longer afraid of the soul-sucking demon.

"I told you, I left it in the crypt," Mary shrugged.

"Give me back the onyx dagger," Eliza hissed between her teeth, her anger growing. "Or so help me, I will not wait for the ceremony to devour your soul."

"That is enough," Elissa stepped up. "The time is ticking by, and these three still have to be prepared."

"Prepared for what?" Sabine asked the blond woman.

"Why, to be our final sacrifices, of course," Amalia sneered. "You and your meddling helped us. We only needed four more souls, and you provided them for us."

"We have decided to keep Sabine, so we need another two powerful souls with enough power to feed ours." Tatum stood next to Amalia. "We think we know where to find them."

"We don't even need your mother's grimoire now. We have your aunt for the incantations and access to Sabine's dagger," Eliza smiled smugly at Sabine, crossing her arms.

Sabine glared back at the woman as the whispers started to echo in Sabine's head once again. Only this time, they were coming from a familiar voice.

"Enough questions," Elissa taunted. "Now, come here and pass me the daggers." Her voice dropped and became melodic.

Mary and Lydia joined hands with each other and Sabine, who stood in front of them, shielding them with her backward outstretched arms. As they joined hands, Sabine whispered to them through her mind, telling them of the plan devised by Kyle and his new soul buddies. Mary and Lydia both telepathically added to the plan.

We are going to need some reinforcements. Mary, can you see to that? Sabine sent her question through her thoughts as Elissa started to sing softly.

"Don't listen," both Mary and Lydia dropped Sabine's hands to cover their ears.

Sabine got caught up in the invisible web Elissa spun with her voice and made the mistake of looking into the woman's eyes.

"Don't worry about them, Sabine," Elissa held Sabine's eyes. "Come to me, Sabine, and I will answer all your questions."

"I will be here for you, Sabine," Tatum stepped up beside Amalia, his eyes turning a deep caramel as Sabine turned her head towards him. Their eyes locked, and he held out his hand.

"That's right, Sabine. You can trust us," Elissa cooed, enticing Sabine.

Ignoring the frantic whispering in her head and staring deep into Tatum's eyes, Sabine took the hand he offered, so he could pull her through the barrier. Tatum pulled her to him. Their eyes still locked, he held her in the circle of his arms, smiling down at her.

"It is such a pity it had to come to this, Sabine," he said to her softly. "I wish you would have come to me on your own accord." He took the cloth with the daggers out of Sabine's hand and gave it to Elissa. "I hope in time you will come to me without any enchantment."

Tatum bent and kissed Sabine gently on the lips. His eyes meeting the enraged ghostly ones of Kyle as he smiled sadistically.

"SABINE," Lydia and Mary screamed. "Fight it, girl. Please, Sabine."

"Sabine, please," Kyle called to her. "Don't do this."

"Sabine will be okay," Lydia said, tightening her lips. "Mary, we have work to do. We need to free all of these souls," she looked towards where Sabine stood. "Kyle, you have to go get the reinforcements. You are the only one who has a way out of here."

"What about Sabine?" Mary asked worriedly.

"Don't you worry about Sabine. I am sure Tatum will take great care of her," Amalia, overhearing Mary's question, mocked spitefully.

THIRTEEN

A Little Help from Friends

Beautiful Sabine," Tatum whispered, still holding her to him.

"Anything for you, Tatum," Sabine told him, still staring into his eyes.

"I'm so glad to hear you say that," Tatum laughed softly down at her. "You see, we need you to find two more preternatural souls for us."

"Of course, Tatum," Sabine told him, "As long as I get to stay near you."

"I would not have it any other way, Sabine," Tatum whispered to her as he bent down towards her and kissed her ear. "I would like to keep you alive, Sabine, so don't let me down."

"I would not want to ever let you down, Tatum," Sabine, mesmerized, stared at Tatum.

"Good," Tatum looked up at Amalia and her sisters, nodding as the three surrounded the grave.

"Amalia and her sisters are going to start the ceremony," Tatum started walking Sabine towards the cemetery gates. "While you and I are going to get those two more preternatural souls."

"I think Marina and her sister Hazel would be best," Sabine smiled shyly at Tatum as they walked towards her car. "Will you come with me?"

"Of course. I won't ever let you out of my sight for too long ever again, my beautiful Sabine," Tatum held open the car door for Sabine.

/ / /

SABINE AND TATUM arrived at Marina's house.

"Now remember, my darling Sabine, you are to get them to come with you," Tatum told her. "We need them alive for this ritual like your aunt and Mary are."

"Of course, Tatum," Sabine smiled and jumped out of the car. "Are you coming with me?"

"You know I am," Tatum followed Sabine to Marina's front door.

After a few rings of the doorbell, Marina answered. She looked sleepy and bedraggled.

"Sabine?" Marina looked confused. "Are you okay?"

"Marina, who is at the door? It is well after eleven." Hazel wandered through, pulling on her fuzzy robe.

"It's Sabine and …" Marina's eyes grew big. "You!" she spat angrily before pulling Sabine inside. "Sabine, get away from him. He is the one I was telling you about."

"Hello again, Marina," Tatum smiled down at the women. "Sabine knows who I am. Don't you, my beautiful Sabine?"

"Yes, Tatum," Sabine turned, held up both hands, magically snaring the sisters. "We need you to come with us."

"Sabine, what are you doing?" Marina shouted at

Sabine as she and her sister were dragged out of their house.

"Marina, what is happening?" Hazel called, fear wobbling her voice. "Sabine, why are you doing this?"

"Tatum needs more preternatural souls," Sabine stared up at him like a lovesick puppy.

"Sabine, listen to me. He has you enthralled. Come on, Sabine. You can break this. You are stronger than this." Marina said with panic in her voice as she and Hazel were forced into the back of Sabine's car.

"I will drive if you like," Tatum held out his hand for the key.

"No, Tatum, that is not safe for you. Let me." Sabine hopped into the car and waited patiently for Tatum to join them. Sabine ignored the pleas and warnings from the two women in the back seat.

"Don't worry. It will all be over soon," Sabine turned and smiled at them.

"You are a monster," Marina kicked at Tatum's seat. "Please let my sister go. She is young. I can find you someone else."

"Marina, please be quiet. I am trying to enjoy this ride with Tatum," Sabine turned and gave Tatum a starry-eyed smile.

*/ */ */

SABINE AND TATUM arrived back at the grave with Marina and Hazel in tow. Tatum pushed the two women through the barrier and onto the grave with Mary, Kyle, and Lydia.

"You two need to be with the rest of the souls I reap tonight," Sabine told them. "Fear not, because it is time for each one of your souls to move on to a better place. I promise you, when I come to reap your souls, you will feel no pain."

"Sabine, what are you doing?" Kyle came to her. "Sabine?" He looked at her frantically.

"Why, soul, you too shall move on soon," Sabine smiled at him. "I am sorry you had to endure an entire day as a lost one."

"Sabine," Lydia shouted at her. "Snap out of it, girl. They have the demon daggers."

"Sabine is no longer on your team," Tatum sneered at Kyle. "After tonight, she would have reaped enough innocent souls to complete all of our transformations and hers."

"What happens when she reaps innocent souls?" Kyle asked, turning to the four women and staring at Sabine, horrified.

"She has to relinquish her claim to the light. Her soul will become dark." Mary said softly. "She will be sent to one of the prison worlds to work towards her rehabilitation."

"Oh no, there will be no prison world for the new light of gold." Tatum grinned at the shocked look on Lydia's, Mary's, and Marina's faces. "Yes, I saw it today when she nearly killed me. We can't have that kind of power go to waste."

"Unlike Nocheli, we think our little Sabine here will be only too glad to share her power with us," Eliza said smugly. "Isn't that right, Tatum?"

"What the hell are they talking about?" Kyle asked, wishing he could punch that smug smile off Tatum's face.

"Nocheli's treacherous family's downfall came when they tried to steal her golden powers," Mary explained. "Nocheli had a feeling her family had been seduced by

The Darkness, so she turned to one of her best friends. A light reaper."

"With the help of the light reaper, Nocheli spelled her children's daggers. Turning each jewel into a prison for her children's souls. Much like the onyx dagger was meant to be for her husband's soul, Marina continued the story. "Especially when she realized he had become The Darkness."

"Only certain reapers have real jeweled daggers," Mary went on. "They are the most powerful reapers born of the golden, silver-blood, or silver-blue light."

"What are those lights?" Kyle asked curiously.

"Golden is the sun, the silver-blood is the blood moon, and the silver-blue is a blue moon," Lydia told Kyle. "But they have to fall on a very specific day and time."

"Nocheli was born of the golden light. Only about two reapers had been born on that day before her, and one other after her." Hazel piped in.

"I thought all reapers have jewels on their daggers?" Kyle looked at Mary.

"Yes, but those are glass, harmless ornaments to make the dagger look pretty," Mary smiled. "The crystals on the demon daggers were made by powerful magic."

"Nocheli's dagger held the sun diamond," Marina continued. "Her dagger could trap a soul, house a soul, and transfer a soul. Along with any power the soul may have."

"With the help of the light reaper, Nocheli was able to trap her children's souls into their daggers. Without a soul, a body dies. Human or preternatural," Mary said, finishing up the story. "Once the souls were trapped, Nocheli went into hiding. Entrusting the daggers, including her own, to six reapers."

"So, there are souls in those daggers?" Kyle asked. "Why do they wear them around their necks?"

"Yes, we believe that until they are fully transformed, part of their soul still remains in the jewel with part of the soul's whose body they are taking over," Hazel said. "It is kind of gross, like body sharing."

"More like body-snatching," Kyle shuddered.

"They have to keep the souls near them," Lydia said. "Or not be apart from them for longer than twenty-four hours at a time, or the body will die, especially as they have not yet completed their demon transformation."

"That is probably why Amalia wanted to snack on you," Hazel laughed at the look on Kyle's face. "She needed to keep that body alive."

"Amalia found a book that had been passed down to our family for generations. Some say it was written by Nocheli herself, about the daggers, and the powers that each amulet possessed," Lydia told Kyle. "The selfish, stupid girl, who has always been obsessed with power, looks, and great wealth was seduced by the story."

"She broke into our house one night and stole the onyx dagger," Mary huffed.

"Both Sabine's mother and father were their generation keepers for two of the daggers," Mary frowned at Lydia for interrupting her story. "So, there were two of the most powerful daggers in the house."

"There are six daggers," Kyle said before asking. "Where are the other two?"

"Well, that cloak you were wearing was one of them." Mary snapped her fingers, and her trusty bag appeared. She opened it to show Kyle the onyx dagger inside of it. "With the black onyx, Amalia could locate the blue, green, amber, and red daggers."

"Tatum was seeing Elissa at the time," Lydia told Kyle.

"The woman used Elissa's thrall to get Tatum to hunt down the reapers in possession of the other daggers."

"He unwittingly reaped their souls. They were the first of the souls to be consumed by the four of them." Mary shuddered at the thought. "Tatum was the one the Council chose to investigate the murders of the reapers. The poor man did not even realize he was investigating himself." Mary and Lydia shook their heads.

"Not until they are full demons can they use their own daggers. That is why Tatum's full essence was not trapped after consuming the first soul. They needed him to reap four more souls." Marina explained. "Each has to consume three souls from the living. Not souls marked for death, but fresh, healthy souls."

"Like mine," Kyle seethed. "Then, they got Sabine to do their dirty work with the three souls below and me."

"Yes," Marina affirmed.

"The duck," Kyle said. "Tatum cut his finger on the blade, and a duck flew at the window. That is when I noticed he went from pretentious jerk to evil jerk."

"They absorb the magic being's power when they absorb their soul," Hazel told Kyle. "Tatum is a pompous jerk, though," Hazel said. "I went to school with the real Tatum, but he had never been evil."

"I don't think Amalia and her horrible sisters realized that the siblings trapped in those daggers are not willing to share their power or lives," Lydia shook her head.

"Not following," Kyle looked at Lydia with a furrowed brow.

"Bit by bit, their own souls are transferred into the demon daggers until they have consumed one of us," Lydia told him. "After the second soul they consume, the host's soul is locked into the amulet. When they consume us, the transformation becomes permanent."

"Now, let's get ready to trap those evil demon souls once and for all," Lydia said, moving everyone into position.

"Sabine is not going to be hurt, right?" Kyle asked, feeling jealous at how close Tatum was standing next to Sabine.

"Sabine will be fine," Lydia said. "You did make sure she put the bracelet on?"

"Yes, I did." Mary nodded.

"One more question," Kyle asked. "Where is the real dagger with the diamond on?"

✦✦✦

"SABINE, where did you put your dagger?" Tatum asked.

"I have it with me, Tatum. Do you need it?" Sabine asked him, worried she had displeased him.

"Oh no, Sabine, as long as you have it with you to help us with the final ritual," he smiled at her.

"Anything for you, Tatum," Sabine sighed as she stared longingly at him.

"Come now, it is time to get started," Tatum took Sabine's hand.

Amalia and her sisters surrounded the grave. They knelt, each taking out their daggers.

Elissa made Lydia start the chanting and the four women, plus Kyle, kneel in front of each of them.

Sabine took her place in the middle of the grave facing Tatum, the magical barrier was taken down.

Midnight arrived. Sabine drew out her dagger that was passed down to her from her mother's ancestors. The diamond on the handle caught the moon's reflection as Sabine held it at the hilt with both hands above her head.

Sabine looked directly at Tatum. He smiled seductively at her.

"You self-inflated jackass," a slow smile spread across Sabine's face, and her eyes turned from hazel to amber.

The ground started to shake, and a breeze blew up from the ground. The whispers of those trapped below them arose loud enough to be heard by all of them.

Tatum, Amalia, Eliza, and Elissa looked up at Sabine.

"Sabine, what are you doing?" Tatum shouted at her. Shock registered on his face as he realized he had been played.

He tried to rush at her, but he found he could not move. Something glinted on Sabine's wrists; it was the mirror hanging from the charm bracelet.

The ground around Tatum and his three demon siblings swirled up into a funnel. This time, the funnel consisted of souls. The souls they had trapped in the grave, waiting to be consumed as a sacrifice to The Darkness. The funnel grew into a wall trapping them.

Tatum, Amalia, Eliza, and Elissa tried to slash the souls with their daggers. As their dagger sliced the air, they found that they were each holding a stick, spelled to resemble the daggers.

Lydia's chanting took on a new tone. Marina, Hazel, Kyle, and Mary followed her. Each of them holding a real demon dagger in their hands. Kyle had the onyx dagger.

Sabine sliced her palm with her dagger, her blood anointed the grave. Lydia dug the blue dagger into the ground in front of Eliza. Mary, Marina, and Hazel did the same with the other daggers.

Kyle dug the onyx dagger into the center of the grave at Sabine's feet. A gold light spread up from Sabine's arms, illuminating the diamond and sending out rays of light to each of the daggers pegged into the ground. The light jumped from the daggers into the heart of Tatum, Amalia, Eliza, and Elissa. They gyrated like they were being shocked by an electric current until the light went out, and each of them slumped to the ground.

The wall of souls spun faster and faster until Sabine knelt, digging her dagger into the dead center of the grave. The jewels in the daggers flickered with a bright light that dulled and went black. A dark veil opened, and the blackness in each jewel was sucked through it. The veil closed, the jewels shattered, then disintegrated into the soil.

The funnel of souls died down as a white veil opened. The five ladies stood and watched the veil collect the souls trapped by the four demons. Sabine's heart felt good as the veil also welcomed the souls of the lost from the cemetery.

When the veil closed, Sabine's heart ached. She dropped down next to Kyle's body. Tears welled up in her eyes. She had not had a chance to say goodbye or ask for his forgiveness.

"I was kind of hoping we could spend what time I have left together." A familiar voice said softly from behind her.

Sabine turned and stood up and threw her arms around his neck.

"How are you here?" Sabine asked him, touching his arms and face. "You are real."

"Sadly, not for long," Kyle smiled, enjoying the feel of her. "Your aunt and her three pals over there worked some mojo, and here I am but only for a few minutes."

"I will take it," Sabine hugged him again.

"Can we go for a walk?" Kyle looked passed her to all the eyes on them. "Also, I am not comfortable around the demon spawn, whether they are cured or not."

///

"NOT THE MOST romantic place in the back seat of your car." Kyle and Sabine laughed. "But, at least it is private."

"Kyle, I am so sorry," Sabine told him, tears sparkling in her hazel eyes. "I hope you can forgive me."

"None of this is your fault, Sabine," Kyle cupped her face. "Your aunt and Mary filled me in on everything while we were stuck in that crypt."

"I wish we had met under different circumstances," Sabine said softly.

"I do too, Sabine. I had to die to find my heart," he looked in her eyes. "I fell in love with you somewhere between yelling at you and going on this crazy adventure with you."

"Oh, Kyle, the moment I knew I would do anything to save you, I realized I had fallen for a ghost," Sabine told him as she pulled his head down to hers. Their lips met in a passionate kiss.

"Maybe in another lifetime, Sabine, you and I will be destined to be together," Kyle smiled. "I need you to do me a favor."

"Anything," she smiled back at him.

Kyle asked her to go to his house and find the jewelry box in his bedside drawer. He wanted her to have it and find a home for Koko, his dog.

"You have a dog?" Sabine asked him, alarmed. "What about food?"

"He has a feeder, but please get him soon," he kissed her again. "Take care, Sabine," Kyle smiled as the veil opened outside the car. Kyle and Sabine got out of the vehicle. As they walked hand and hand towards it, Kyle faded into his ghostly form.

FOURTEEN

Second Chances

Sabine stood at the bottom of the stairs looking up at Kyle's cabin. It was hard to believe it had only been twenty-eight hours ago that she had first climbed these stairs.

The cabin was exactly as they had left it. The only light that shone in the house was the one left on in the kitchen. Sabine stopped at the kitchen door and looked into it. The broken coffee cup still lay on the floor. Sabine wanted to go and clean it up, but she knew she could not. The cleanup crew would come through and do their thing.

Walking through the house, Sabine stopped to look at the pictures on the wall. Her heart stopped and started to beat in her throat. Most of them were of Kyle and a little girl. Fear gripped Sabine. Had Kyle had a daughter?

Sabine rushed through to his bedroom, looking in the drawers for the music box. She found out in the bottom drawer. It looked like it had been well-loved and completely bedazzled except for the engraving, To Jody, My Heart. She ran her fingers over the engraved letters; a feeling of sorrow touched her. There was a lot of pain here. A slight whisper tickled Sabine's ears. Closing her eyes, Sabine held the box and listened.

Tears spilled from her eyes. She now knew why Kyle had locked himself away. She opened the box. Inside was a picture of Jody and a large dog. Something touched her foot from beneath the bed, and Sabine froze. Rats, there better not be rats. Sabine bravely looked beneath the bed and got a face full of slobber.

"Koko, I presume," she laughed, wiping dog slobber from her cheeks as a huge Tibetan Mastiff squeezed out from under the bed. He hopped up next to her and put his head on her lap. He knew his owner was gone, as was his little girl. "Hey boy, I know what you are going through."

She scratched his ears, put the picture back in the jewelry box, and stood up. "Look, Koko, I am not sure how this will work, but do you want to come home with me?"

Koko barked, jumping excitedly from the bed.

"I am going to take that as a yes then," Sabine took the jewelry box. "So, I take it these things belong to you?" Sabine looked around the cabin for Koko's things and made a few trips to the car juggling food bowls, food, toys, and a large dog bed.

"Goodbye, Kyle. I hope you find Jody where you are now," She drove out of his driveway.

"HERE SHE COMES," Mary watched from the sitting room window. "Are you going to tell her how Kyle offered to hide the daggers or that you have him entombed here. In the family crypt?"

"When she is ready, Mary," Lydia said, shaking her head. She watched Sabine letting her gigantic furry passenger out of the car. "Looks like you are getting a new housemate, Mary," Lydia laughed as Mary swore.

///

"WHAT THE HECK IS THAT?" Mary stood at the top of the stairs of Sabine's family home with her hands on her hips, staring at the big animal.

Koko barked, bounded up the stairs, and headed straight for Mary. He nearly knocked her over as he jumped up to greet her and cover her face with dog kisses.

"Down, you big brute," Mary fended off the animal. "Sit!" she said in a voice that made both Lydia and Sabine want to sit.

Koko sat, staring lovingly at Mary.

"If you are going to live here, there are rules," she told Koko. "Now come along, everyone. Let's go get some tea." She turned, but Koko did not move. "You too, big guy."

Koko barked and took off after Mary.

"You went for a jewelry box and came back with a dog?" Lydia laughed.

"I could not leave him there," Sabine told Lydia about Jody as they followed Mary into the kitchen.

"Hello, Sabine," a deep voice came from inside the kitchen.

Sabine froze, her eyes meeting Tatum's.

"What is he doing here, and why are you letting him near my dog?" Sabine said, crossly watching Tatum pat Koko.

"Now Sabine," Mary said sternly. "It is not the lad's fault he was possessed by a demon."

"That does not answer why he is in my house?" Sabine exhaled.

"We are making sure he is properly rehabilitated. And

as you are taking time off to find out what you want to do with your life," Mary gestured, "we thought you two could get to know each other again."

"No, absolutely not," Sabine stormed out the backdoor.

Her swing at the bottom of the garden hung from a tree at the edge of a lake. It was her peaceful place.

"Sabine," Tatum said from behind her. "I won't stay if it makes you uncomfortable."

"Okay."

"I am sorry for everything that's happened," Tatum watched her swing. "I always pictured our first real meeting to be a lot different than it turned out to be." He was about to leave her alone when she spoke.

"Tatum," Sabine turned towards him, her eyes conveying her mistrust and dislike. "You can stay. But you and I, getting to know each other?" In her mind, she saw Tatum as a manipulating two-faced demon wanting to rob her of her powers. Not to mention the parts where he and those deranged sisters tried to hurt her loved ones. "I don't see that happening soon, if ever."

"Understood," Tatum nodded. But before he walked off, he said, "Thank you for letting me stay, Sabine." It was not going to be easy winning back her trust, but it would be worth it in the end. Tatum was sure.

"I guess everyone deserves a second chance," Sabine smiled down at the picture of Kyle's handsome face she had taken from his house.

About the Author

Renee Joiner has been in love with the supernatural for longer than she can remember, so it is no surprise that she is an author of paranormal urban fantasy. Although she discovered her passion for writing when she was only twelve years old, she didn't make her writing debut until many years into the future. Adventurous and fun-loving, she enjoys traveling to new places, exploring new sights and meeting new people. Thus, she delights in creating fantastical worlds that are sure to give her readers an escape from the real world while simultaneously providing thrilling entertainment.

Besides her special knack for writing, you'll also find a passion for metaphysics spirituality which she has been nurturing for over four decades. Renee hails from New York and currently resides with her husband in their empty nest—unless you count their three adorable fur babies—in Florida. She enjoys adding to her sea of knowledge and thus spends her free time learning new things.

To find out more about Renee Joiner, feel free to visit her **official website**.

facebook.com/reneejoinerauthor

twitter.com/iamreneejoiner

instagram.com/reneejoinerauthor

amazon.com/author/reneejoiner

Book Series by Renee

Thorne Sisters Chronicles
Possessed by Magic
Reincarnated by Magic
Immortal by Magic

Thank You..

Thank you for reading my book!
I really appreciate all of your feedback and I love to hear what you have to say. Please leave your review at your favorite retailer!